TEN STORIES

YOU SHOULD READ BEFORE THEY BECOME MOVIES

MIKE SLOSBERG

TEN STORIES YOU SHOULD READ BEFORE THEY BECOME MOVIES

Mike Slosberg

Nightengale Press

TEN STORIES YOU SHOULD READ BEFORE THEY BECOME MOVIES

If you find a typo in this book, know it is intentional since only God is perfect.

Library of Congress Cataloging-in-Publication Data
Slosberg, Mike,
TEN STORIES YOU SHOULD READ
BEFORE THEY BECOME MOVIES/ Mike Slosberg
ISBN 13: 978-1-945257-44-5
eBook
Genre: Short Story

Published in the United States of America
©2023
Nightengale Press
www.nightengalepress.com

July 2023
10 9 8 7 6 5 4 3 2 1

INTRODUCTION

A publisher friend, upon hearing the title of my book felt the declaration that the stories could be made into movies was presumptuous and a bit pretentious.

I tried to explain that the real measure of a good movie idea has little to do with its length. Short stories have inspired some of the best movies: Rear Window, Field of Dreams, Apocalypse Now—just three examples plucked from a quick GOOGLE search. There are dozens and dozens more.

Ideas are ideas. Good or bad, they don't come in lengths like pants.

A short story is a tight compression of thought that not only reads well on the page but can, in many cases, also be expanded and dramatically translated into a motion picture.

In other words, the only relevant criterion for a good movie idea—is a good idea.

That's why I decided to toss ten of my stories into the mosh pit of potential cinematic fodder, and let the quality of the stories, not their length, be the determining factor.

I hope you enjoy reading them, and possibly seeing them someday on the big or small screen.

Film rights are available.

For Janet, my greatest fan and toughest critic.

STORY I
THE FOX AND THE LADY

THE FOX AND THE LADY

I've never been in prison.

Of course, I've read about prisons.

But truth be told, my most indelible impressions of what prisons really look like come from the movies.

For my money, It's not really a prison unless it looks like the ones in those old James Cagney movies. You know, a huge gray stone Gothic fortress, with armed guards in towers, razor wire and searchlights. And a steel front entrance so gigantic and imposing that it needs a human-size steel door built into it, like a tiny mouse hole in a large wall.

The particular prison I found myself standing in front of—a so-called minimum security, white-collar joint--looked more like a neighborhood Community Center. It was a Lego-like jumble of cinder blocks covering the top of a large dirt hill like a badly fitted hairpiece. A black-top parking lot spread out below it like a large oil stain under a leaking used car. Thirty-nine steps led up from the parking lot to the entrance. By the 39th we are both breathing hard.

I was here at this prison to accompany my best friend -- who happened to also be my lawyer, so he wouldn't be alone, as he began serving a two-year sentence.

The convicting jury, after nodding-off through punishingly-boring testimony, unanimously agreed that his starched white collar had a dirty ring around it.

THE FOX AND THE LADY

Thanks to an unusual and generous act of professional courtesy, my friend had been granted special permission by the court to report to prison on his own recognizance, and today was delivery day.

Once inside, an arrow painted on the floor directs us toward a beat-up, gray-metal desk. Planted behind it, a dumpster-size guard -- a muscular black man who looks like he was born wearing his skin-tight uniform shirt and never stopped growing into it.

Beyond the stoic guard, a large, over-heated room is filled with an odd assortment of benches, chairs and tables, and it is overflowing with prisoners and visitors. This bizarre diorama resides in a thick, yellowish fog of stale cigarette smoke.

A bulletin board across one long wall explodes in a jumble of notices, greeting cards, children's drawings and schematics illustrating proper procedures in the event of choking, bleeding, rioting inmates and heart attacks. On the wall opposite the bulletin board, stand a half dozen vending machines, ready to spit out stale coffee, overpriced candy, stale sandwiches and room temperature soft drinks.

The prisoners are dressed in an odd assortment of surplus WWII army work fatigues. The visitors—mostly women—are each trying their damnedest to look adoringly, or at least pleasantly, at their respective felons. An assortment of snot-streaked babies sucked on bottles, pacifiers, or just scream their heads off. Older kids wandered around, oozing a level of boredom rooted in one-too-many visiting days.

A floor-to-ceiling picture window offered a sweeping view of the depressingly bleak, monochromatic, countryside of Pennsylvania in February. Several prisoners can be seen walking the footpaths outside, heads down, moving slowly, showing an indifference to time, which the military and penal institutions seem to cultivate so effectively.

THE FOX AND THE LADY

Ironically, the double-wide, lethargic guard has never experienced a prisoner actually attempting to come into the prison —not, at least, without being securely cuffed to a U.S. Marshal. This puzzling "penal anomaly" seems to baffle the buffalo size guard and for one gloriously tricky moment it looked like we might get tossed out on a technicality.

So, we just stood there, visiting hours in full swing, trying to check-in, as if we're at the front desk of some cheesy motel.

Finally, after lots of back-and-forth phone conversations between the guard and God-only-knows, my friend is finally allowed entry.

As they led him away, he looked physically ill and, understandably, scared to death. I was politely ordered to wait, informed he'd be brought out to say goodbye — but not before he was processed, and outfitted in his prison garb.

Walking beside him I said, "I'm right here, buddy…okay? Take your time…I'm not going anywhere," trying to assure him, as he was shuffled to the far side of a thick, finger-smudged glass door — no doubt, bullet–and maybe bomb-proof, as well.

I finally found an empty chair and settled in for a long wait. A dog-eared Orientation Pamphlet caught my eye. Leafing through, I am informed, by several badly written pages, that my friend isn't physically ill or scared half to death -- he is simply deep into what is technically called, "Surrender Shock." But even I, without benefit of medical training can see that this is just a fancy way of saying he is physically ill and scared half to death!

For the next hour I drank bad vending machine coffee, people-watched, and read the dumb Orientation booklet so many more times I started to actually like it.

And then…I saw *him*!

THE FOX AND THE LADY

The Silver Fox!

The very sight of him here, in this place, was so unexpected, so startling that I begin to choke on my coffee. The rhino-size guard instantly materialized from behind his desk and pounded my back, hard—but not quite hard enough to cause internal bleeding.

Son of a bitch! The Silver Fox! After all the years, he was almost the way I remembered him. A bit shopworn, needing a shave, but even in the cheap army duds he had class. He was still The Fox.

I watched as he stood, patiently waiting on the far side of the very same door my friend had been hauled through.

Seeing The Fox again, in this place, floods me with vivid memories of the Bel Air Hotel. A mind-picture so vivid, I'm tempted to squint, just remembering the blinding glare of hot California sun as it bounces off the mirrored surface of the hotel's pool.

In my opinion, the Bel Air is the classiest hotel in the Western Hemisphere. I experience joy just driving to it from the LA Airport. With radio blasting, I drive North on the San Diego Freeway, hanging a right onto the Sunset Boulevard exit ramp, then head east, and next to the UCLA campus and, a little farther up, negotiate the tricky left-hand turn into the huge gates that separate Bel Air from the rest of the world.

It's not as if Bel Air is a town. It's not. Bel Air is more like a neighborhood.

One consisting of the most expensive and exclusive private estates in earth. It's the place people move, to escape the relative poverty of places like Monaco, Aspen, Palm Beach and, of course, Beverly Hills.

THE FOX AND THE LADY

And sitting smack in the middle of Bel Air, the "neighborhood" is Bel Air, the Hotel.

A valet takes your car. A charming footbridge takes you across a curving, water-filled moat, leading to a theatrically manicured jungle of palm trees, thick bushes and exotic tropical ferns. The sweet smell of eucalyptus is the signature scent and there are a bevy of swans gliding along the mote, as well as a flamboyance of pink flamingos. Real ones, not the plastic one's you might find propped up in front of a mobile home.

I first laid eyes on The Fox years ago, at the Bel Air hotel during the early sixties, when anyone connected with film or TV commercial production could "live large" thanks to No-Questions-Asked expense accounts.

My work required my staying at the Bel Air for weeks at a time. I was what is called in the hotel trade as, "A friend of the house." Even so, at the Bel Air, that didn't buy very much. The front-desk staff knew me by name, and treated me with the respect afforded to frequent, albeit non-celebrity guests. I knew damned well they saved their more refined level of obsequiousness for the wheat and not the chaff.

The nature of my work—reading scripts, building film budgets, shuffling through endless location photos—made the hotel pool the ideal, sunny location to conduct my daily business. It was a whisper-quiet space, surrounded by more of the thick, and meticulously tended tropical greenery. Lounging there, alone—surprisingly, it was sparsely used—always made me feel special, like I was nestled inside a priceless Faberge egg.

THE FOX AND THE LADY

It was while working at the pool that I first saw The Silver Fox. He wasn't The Fox then. That was the name I gave him some time later. In fact, I never did learn his actual name.

To me, he was just The Fox.

He was a handsome man who looked to be in his early forties. He could have been ten or twenty years older, but certainly looked much younger. He stood about six foot with thick, prematurely silver hair — hence the nickname.

He was dark complexioned, with high cheekbones—a little Native American looking, but not so much, as would turn any heads in a Presbyterian Church.

It was clear to me that The Fox had some money. Everything about him seemed the kind of perfect that money buys. The gold Rolex, the Gucci attaché and horse-bit loafers, the beautiful swim clothes, the soft leather notebooks he worked from. It was all so damned perfect. The tan was always there, too. His nails manicured. All twenty of them. Everything, like I said, was pure perfection.

However, I would be lying if I didn't admit that, at the time, it wasn't The Fox who first caught my eye, but rather the drop-dead gorgeous lady who accompanied him. She was also perfection: like if there was a human female version of a gold Rolex. That would be her.

The Fox and The Lady had a routine. They would arrive at the pool about ten in the morning, walking arm in arm, along the path that was still wet from the early morning's automatic sprinkling. The plants, so meticulously tended, would brush them in benediction as they passed, as if the touching would somehow bring the plants good fortune.

As I noted, the Lady was a pure fantasy. Possibly twenty-five, certainly no older. Hair so damn black that it looked blue and any fool could see that it soaked up the heat from the sun and must have felt thick and warm to the touch. She was tall. Almost to The Fox's eyebrows. But that was in sandals, so in heels, I imagined they must have been eye to eye. Her body was like everything else The Fox owned. To call it perfection, falls short. So whatever female image comes to your mind as being absolutely perfect—double that.

Strangely, it was her teeth that got to me. Even from across the pool they melted me. Large and white and framed with full, soft looking lips that smiled and laughed and whispered and did all sorts of marvelous things that were just barely legal in public, at the side of a pool. Even at the Bel Air.

As I said, they would always arrive, arm in arm. Behind them a waiter would be wheeling the food, arranged on a service cart. The polished silver and glassware, were blinding with reflections from the sunlight.

The waiter would set up their table and then, somehow turn himself into a plant or something, and disappear. I would sit across the pool, trying to relish the scene, unobserved behind my RayBans.

Over the months and months of my observing The Fox and The Lady, I got to know their habits quite well.

They took their coffee black and their croissants warm, with fresh butter and English jam. Every so often they would have thick slices of French toast, and once, after what I can only assume was a particularly strenuous evening, they each consumed an order of steak and eggs.

Each time they completed a meal the waiter would materialize with a fresh pot of hot coffee and clear the breakfast things.

They had this wonderfully romantic organization of the outdoor furniture. Two chaise lounges rafted together, head to foot. So all they needed to do to see one another was glance up. The shortest distance between two points. On a small table, between them, they'd arrange their simple needs. The lotions, the books. On the opposite side, next to him on a second table were his attaché, his notebooks—and whatever else was necessary to pursue his particular commerce.

In the hours that followed, The Fox would work. The lady would read books, nap and take the sun. Solid hours of that... and of frequent touching and stroking; of casual kissing of each other's toes, of glances that had texture and dimension; of romantic vibrations, so powerful, they damn near rattled the ice cubes in my Fresca.

And the whole scene was right there, unfolding right between the vee formed by my imported Japanese rubber flip-flops. Within that wedge of space, I was witnessing, and fantasizing about, one of the great love affairs of all time.

For early afternoon meals, the waiter would set a table under the shade of a giant white umbrella. Sometimes they had a salad, served in a gigantic wooden bowl and chopped, and tossed at the table, Hollywood style.

Other times there were large club sandwiches and bowls of iced Crenshaw melon and plum size strawberries. And, of course, a chilled bottle of white wine within reach. And always fresh cut flowers. The Fox and The Lady were both hearty eaters. Obviously not dieters, they would pack it all away with great gusto.

Under the table there was always a lot of silliness going on with their feet and legs. At times, though not often, I felt as though I was eavesdropping. However, I never once saw them look in my direction, or even seem to notice that I was there at all.

After lunch they would nap for an hour, always mixed with the occasional toe kissing, touching and meaningful looking. Then into the pool. The Lady never wore a cap and her hair, soaking wet, was even more exciting than when it was when dry.

Thanks to my Polaroid lenses, I could catch the action under the water, just like in the television commercials. But the details were not important. It was all so wholesomely erotic—not in the least smutty or crude.

They were in love. Anyone could tell.

By five they were heading back to their rooms. Arm in arm. Hair matted and dried by the sun. Skin glowing and warm.

I never saw them in the evening. Not once in the hotel's bar or restaurant or entering a limousine on the parking lot side of the little mote or feeding the pink flamingos. But the next day, if they were still at the hotel, they would appear, and the routine would repeat itself.

I saw them many times. Not on every trip, but on many. In cooler weather they would appear poolside wearing expensive looking sweaters and carefully tailored French jeans.

Once, when I missed them, I inquired. Not to the assistant manager…all he would give me would be a circumspect passport-photo look. But there was a friendly and chatty telephone operator who always traded gossip with me – due, I suspect, to the fresh H&H bagels I would frequently schlep from New York, and present to her.

The man, she told me, came from Texas. At least that's where his phone calls came from. The Lady's calls, on the other hand, were always from Chicago. The routine, according to my friendly operator, was predictably consistent. He would call for reservations from Texas. Confirm a suite for himself and put a hold on an adjoining room. Within the hour, a call from Chicago would book the room that had been put on hold.

The lady would arrive a day before The Fox and leave a day after. She would call the morning of her arrival and arrange for a limousine to meet her at the airport, and transport her to the hotel. Once checked in, she would give a detailed list to the bell captain indicating how she wanted The Fox's rooms stocked. Apparently, he took a suite that had a kitchen and she would order special treats to stock the refrigerator. From what the telephone lady had heard, The Fox was, among other things, very big on Baskin Robbins Chocolate Almond and always had plenty sent in.

The Fox would arrive the following morning.

The procedure was always the same and—at least at the Bel Air—had been going on for almost four years.

'Except in August," she added.

I raised my shoulders, palms up, as if to ask, So? What's with August?

The telephone lady looked to her right and left, as if someone else could possibly have fit into the cramped space she occupied, along with her phone equipment.

"If they're on the same schedule as every other year, it should happen next week."

"What should happen next week?"

"Will you be here next week?" she whispered.

"I don't know," I whispered back.

"If you're here, you'll see. If you're not, you won't."

And that was that. I could have strangled a baby flamingo in front of her but not another bit of information would have passed her lips.

She just laughed and repeated, "If you're here next week, you'll see, and if not, you won't."

I barely managed to make it the next week. As it was, I had to decimate my schedule and tell several punishable-by-death lies to my best client. But I made it. The telephone lady was off duty by the time I checked in. The night manager, when I asked, in a very discrete way, about The Fox, looked at me with an alarmed expression, as if I had exposed my private parts. I quickly went to my room and tried to sleep, praying for sunshine.

At 9:30 I was at my spot across the pool. I polished off a rasher of bacon and two fried eggs. I dunked what was left of an English muffin into a second cup of coffee

And then I saw him.

Or was it him?

At first, I couldn't be certain.

The glare off the white cloth covering the serving cart, the silver service and glassware was all blindingly familiar.

And it looked like the Fox…but different.

A little less postured. Stooped a bit, actually. His hair was sleep disheveled and sticking up in the back. The rest was the same. Gucci case—that sort of thing.

Then out of the glare stepped—The Lady? A lady!

Attractive, in a middle age sort of way, but pudgy and wearing a less-than-flattering, yet sensible, one-piece swim outfit. The kind with a little pleated skirt. Marching directly under the skirt, milk white legs showing the first, faint hint of criss-crossing blue veins.

They sat across from each other at the table the waiter had set for breakfast. The Fox was served a short stack of pancakes and sausages, toast and coffee. She expertly evicted two soft-boiled eggs into a bowl and ate them slowly, along with one slice of rye toast.

They sat all that morning on lounge chairs facing the sun. There wasn't a lot of conversation. He worked from a table between them. She read and occasionally did something with a needle, thread and a small round wooden frame. Much of the time she spent looking straight ahead while supporting a gull-wing cardboard sun reflector under her chin.

At noon there was a hamburger for him and a cottage cheese and fruit thing for her. They read for another hour and then doggy-paddled silently around the pool a few times. She wore a zeppelin-shaped swimming cap that snapped over her lacquered hair, which was a shade of blue-gray usually associated with a much older woman, but quite well done and rather attractive.

By five they had left the pool area.

A month later I was back at the Bel Air and so was The Silver Fox. Once again, with The Lady.

Once the realization hit me, I felt real pain for the man. For eleven months out of the year he had this luscious child, flying out to meet him and kiss his toes and everything. And then in August he had the blue-haired, pudgy wife. The one that probably worked her tail off while he went through university, or gave him all her father's oil money—or God knows what.

But I knew my preference. I loved The Lady and resented the wife. With lady he was The Silver Fox! With the wife, he was just another rich guy with gray hair. I cherished The Fox and The Lady.

And now here, in this cockamamie prison, I'm seeing him once again. Not poolside at the Bel Air, but in this stinking minimum-security prison in Nowhere, Pennsylvania. Wearing worn and faded prison clothes. The leather of his faithful Gucci shoes a bit scuffed, and his face a day past needing a shave. But he still looked really good.

THE FOX AND THE LADY

Then it struck me. Of course! The lady. The visitor who's here to see him must be the beautiful black-haired lady. My heart pounds in anticipation of seeing her again. Her smile. Her body. Those teeth!

My eyes search the room, visually shoving people aside, moving in for close-ups, yearning to recognize her. I pan past the vending machines, deep into corners of the room.

And then I see her! It's the hair. Who could forget?

The Fox comes into the main room. His face cuts into the smile I saw so many times. In an instant they are meshed into each other's arms.

Her hair presses against the cheap fabric of his ratty army coat.

She's a bit heavier than I remember and finally closer to an age more in keeping with the blue-gray color of her hair. The milk white, blue veined legs are now covered with neat, dark flannel slacks.

They walk holding each other to a corner where they find an empty table and she opens a food hamper and goes about dealing with its contents.

He reaches in and retrieves a small salami and laughs. She hands him the prison-mandated plastic utensils, and opens a "pull top" tin of pate. He cuts off a bit of salami and feeds it to her and then takes her hand and kisses it. My mind computes pictures, cutting back and forth, past to present. At the Bel Air pool, he kissed the lady's toes…and now his wife's fingertips. Toes, fingertips. Then and now. The level of passion seems to be the same. I should have known he would end up with her in his time of need.

Just then, my friend is brought back into the room. He looks terrible. He's obviously still in Surrender Shock. Sick and scared.

Standing there in his prison garb, his eyes glazed, I could clearly see the embarrassment he is feeling. That I should see him looking like a forty-five-year-old private in some defeated comic army is almost too much for him.

I grab his arm and pull him over to one of the vending machines. His tongue is chalk-white and his blood apparently has succumbed to the laws of gravity, pouring from his body, into his legs.

I can't leave him this way.

"Hey, look at me. Remember I told you about The Silver Fox?"

"Oh my God, look at me," he mumbles. His face is in his hands.

I pull his hands away from his face. "Listen. Listen to me! The clothes...you look fine, don't worry. Remember I told you...about The Silver Fox? At the hotel? He's here, right here!"

"Oh my God, look at me. No, DON'T...I look like a bum. A crazy bum."

His head is back in his hands again but I can see he's starting to look at me through the narrow spread of his fingers.

"Remember I told you about the guy at the hotel? The Silver Fox?"

"The...guy...from the...pool? At the Beverly Hills?"

"No, not the Beverly Hills. The Bel Air." I was starting to get through to him.

"Oh, yeah...the Bel Air," he said. His hands were off his face. Some color started creeping back to his face.

"He's here! Right here! And—he's not a visitor," I said in a triumphant whisper.

My friend looked around the room. "He's in the pokey, too? I didn't know they could put you away for adultery."

I forced a laugh at his bad joke because it was pulling his mind away from the shame and humiliation of prison.

"Where is he?"

I pointed discreetly to the corner with a quick incline of my head. My friend's eyes followed the gesture. "Where?"

"Look, see...he's over there."

"The gray-haired guy with the salami?"

I moved my head up and down. "Listen...get to know him, okay?"

"I don't see any wild looking lady with him. Where is she?"

"Not here," I said, looking down at my feet.

He looked puzzled, "Then who...OH NO! Don't tell me he's here with the blue hair wife you told me about?" he said, a touch too loudly.

I saw the big guard's arm flex under the desk at the sound of a raised voice. Maybe it wasn't such a minimum-security place after all.

"Shhh...not so loud," I said. "Yeah, he's here with the wife. Try, you know, to get to know him."

"Oh, wow! I'd really like to see that other lady," he laughed. "Even wearing this crappy outfit, I'd like that..."

We were both laughing now, each with tears in our eyes. It's called tension release.

"Why...should I ...get...to know...him?"

"So...you...can..." I had trouble getting the words out past the laughing.

"So...I can...what?"

"So you can find out who she is. Then I can go to Chicago and see her myself."

"So you can what?" He barked hysterically.

The black arm shot under the desk again.

"Shhhhh..." I said, finger sawing up and down across my lips.

"Yeah, I can look her up. What's wrong with that?"

"Listen, schmuck! If I ever get The Lady's name, I'm KEEPING it…and when I get out, I'M GOING TO LOOK HER UP…" He was laughing but, more importantly, he was a little more like his normal self.

And then the big guard was gently leading my friend away. He knew, bless that sliver of his humanity, how tough the first day could be.

Right up to the glass door my friend is still laughing.

"I'M LOOKING HER UP WHEN I GET OUT…AND DON'T YOU FORGET IT…I WOULDN'T GIVE YOU HER NAME ON A BET."

He was like a funny drunk but his eyes were clear and I knew he would be okay. He was far too smart not to grab onto The Silver Fox story to help him out from under his depression.

I was also directed to leave.

The cold, clear air was refreshing after so many hours in the prison's overheated and smoky reception area.

As I picked my way across the ice-spotted parking lot toward my car, I saw the door of a brown Mercedes swing open.

A Gucci attaché got out.

The briefcase wasn't as new as I remembered. But the lady holding it was and she was just as lovely.

I knew it! Even from prison, the old Fox had pulled it off. But now his timing was a little bit rusty and I couldn't bear the thought of it all crumbling down around him. Not now. Not while in prison.

So, I took a deep breath and approached her. "Hi there. This is going to sound silly but a long time ago, at the pool of the Bel Air Hotel…"

She looked at me carefully for a moment and then recognition spread like a blush across her incredibly beautiful face.

"Oh, yes," she smiled, "I do remember you…other side of the pool. Rubber flip-flops. We used to call you…" She paused for a second, grabbing for the memory. "THE PALE PEEPER!" She laughed—God, those teeth!—and said, "So, what are you doing here?"

I touched her arm and said, "If you'll allow me to buy you a cup of coffee, I'll tell you why you might want to wait until tomorrow to see your friend."

And tell her I did.

STORY II
THE LAST MARBLE

THE LAST MARBLE

It was Sarah's first time in Atlantic City and everything she saw and heard thrilled her. The ocean, its waves endlessly pounding the broad sandy beach. The huge colorful umbrellas and swooping gray and white seagulls, endlessly gliding in their hunt for food. The wide, seemingly endless boardwalk, alive with throngs of happy people. The shops, arcades, and entertainment piers. The fashionably dressed couples riding in big rattan rolling chairs, each being pushed by sweating, dark skinned men.

On such a day, who could imagine that America is only months away from the turbulence of the Great Depression—the initial step in the long, painful march toward a second World War.

The Bird of Paradise is a high-class Assisted Living facility. Originally, a pre-war co-op, the high-rise building was converted into an expensive and comfortable home for the elderly. The accommodations include studios, one- and two-bedroom apartments and a separate "total care" wing that is more like a hospital with single private rooms, and a full medical staff.

The "Bird"—as it's called by most—is filled with the elderly who can afford a first-class ticket for their trip to eternity. Some guests—they are all called guests—are those who no longer can, or wish, to live alone. Others are placed there by wealthy, guilt-ridden children who want to park their senior charges in a facility posh enough to ease their conscience. Regardless of motivations, the intent is to know a loved one is safely out of the way and cared for in one of God's classier and well-furnished waiting rooms.

It was almost too wonderful for young Sarah to bear. And now, to make the day more amazing, to have a real date—her very first one alone, with a boy—it was just extraordinary.

The boy, Morris Blinderman, was sixteen—not quite a year older than Sarah. He was in Atlantic City visiting his first cousin, Ida Blinderman, Sarah's best girlfriend. Morris was from St. Louis and Ida had confided to Sarah that the Mid-West branch of the Blinderman clan was very, very poor.

Morris was a nice-looking boy—thin without being skinny, with thick, jet-black hair. He was about an inch shorter than Sarah and, like Sarah, this was his first visit to Atlantic City. Actually, his first trip outside the city limits of St. Louis. And Sarah was the first girl he had ever taken out on anything even resembling a real date. He had never been so nervous.

Penrod's cell phone—blasting the special ringtone dedicated to calls from his sister, Shelly—rudely violates his thrice-weekly deep-tissue massage.

He hesitates for several rings, steeling himself to endure another, '*...why don't you ever call about Mom*' conversation. He finally taps the switch on his Bluetooth ear bud.

"Hey, sister. Good news or bad news?" Penrod says, his voice muffled a bit by the thick Turkish towels surrounding his face.

"As if you give a shit, fuckface," Shelly says.

"If you're about to drop another guilt-trip on me, Shell, I don't have time for it. I'm up to my neck in turtle-shit. Three of my best clients had green-lighted projects, then yesterday every fucking one was put on indefinite hold. In this town that means, 'Dead Movie Walking.' So, when you tell me whatever you're going to tell me —be gentle and please don't yell."

Shelly, barely controlling her anger, "You know damned well what I'm going to tell you. I'm dealing with all the fucking problems of our mother who will soon be turning ninety-two. Granted, in the world of longevity, it's a blessing, but in day-to-day practice, it's a fucking curse. I barely managed when we moved her in with me. No fun or games here, Penny. None whatsoever. (PAUSE) For your information, our mother is totally bat-shit. Believe me, Penny, I'm grateful you're coughing up the bucks for the fancy-schmancy joint in which we've parked her but, face facts. I'm the one here every day putting in the sweat equity. I have no life. I have Uber on speed dial. And if you don't get back here real soon—like right away—uh, you might as well...I don't know, maybe just stay in California, and send one of those little stuffed bears dressed up like a Hollywood Agent, with your name on it. Because I swear, the way her mind is disintegrating, if I say that little cuddly Teddy is you, I guarantee she'll believe it is. And you won't even have to buy a plane ticket."

"Christ, Shell, it's not like I live in the Village and can just hop a subway when I want to see her. I've a business to run. And, besides,

I was there not so long ago—yah know, on my way to---I forget, London or Paris—anyway—uh, she looked great. Knew who I was. Was sharp as a tack. Asked about my job and how I liked California."

"Penny, get real for fuck's sake, that was six months ago! In dementia years, that's a lifetime. And granted, for someone her age, she does look good. But what is euphemistically called her mind is rapidly leaving earth's orbit and heading into outer space."

(LONG PAUSE/SILENCE/BREATHING)

Finally, Penny breaks the silence. "How's Pop dealing with all this? Does Mom recognize him…know who he is?"

"Know who he is? Of course, she knows who he is. Yesterday she knew he was Pop's brother, Alvin, who died fifteen years ago. And this morning, as I was wheeling her from the dining room pop arrived, and she knew he was the FedEx guy and cursed him for not delivering whatever the fuck she believes she ordered."

"Okay, look, Shell, you're right. The truth? I hate seeing you upset like this. I will come out. How 'bout, I move some stuff around and shoot for this weekend. Is that good? Pencil me in for Friday, okay? I'll call when I know the flight details. (PAUSE) I love you, Shell, and I'm truly sorry you have to be the tip of the spear on this."

(SARCASTIC) "Yea, me, too, Penny. Me too."

At precisely nine in the morning, Morris Blinderman called for Sarah at her apartment—a third-floor walkup rented by her father for the family's first two-week summer vacation, away from Philadelphia.

Sarah's mother had packed a lunch for them—two cream

cheese and jelly sandwiches carefully wrapped in waxed paper, two apples, and as a special treat to share: a Hershey bar. At the last minute she added two nickels so Sarah and Morris could each buy a Coke.

Just knowing her brother will arrive in a few days has eased the pressure of Shelly's unending chore of being the sole companion for her rapidly deteriorating, nonagenarian mother.

The call with Penny is a good end to hectic day, and by the time Shelly is back to her apartment it's almost ten o'clock. All she wants is a hot shower and a large glass of Bourbon.

Thirty minutes later she's in the living room, relaxed and wrapped in a thick terry robe sipping a Jack Daniel's and trying–without success–to find something to watch on TV.

After a second drink, Shelly decides to go through some of her mother's things. In the back of her mom's bedroom closet, Shelly finds a box filled with old photos and mementos. Some are pictures she's seen before over the years, but there are other items she never saw before: ticket stubs to music events, a dried corsage, never-before-seen family snapshots, concert programs and playbills, ancient birthday and valentine cards from her and Penny when they were youngsters, little stacks of letters, each tied in ribbons and some yellowing playbills from long-forgotten Broadway shows.

Morris carried the little lunch bag as they walked the two blocks east, to the ocean, then south, along the boardwalk. The

wide beach was packed with people, a seemingly unbroken stain of black bathing costumes running from the boardwalk directly into the sea. Large umbrellas provided shade for blankets spread with food hampers. Happy children ran through the mass, scattering wakes of sand, their high-pitched shouts mixed with the crash of waves and screech of gulls.

Shelly slept later than usual, thanks to a slight Bourbon hangover. After breakfast and a long soak in a hot tub, she girds herself for another long day with Mom. On the way out of the apartment and on a whim, she decides to take along the box of things she found in her mother's closet. Going through its contents together will help pass the time.

Shelly arrives while the guests are having their lunch in the dining room. She sees Sarah sitting with three other women. Shelly watches as her mother maneuvers the food around on her plate, making it seem as if she has eaten a bit of everything—without needing to ingest much more than a few morsels.

Sarah and Morris strolled the boardwalk, passing block after block of shops, until, finally, they reached their destination: The World Famous Steel Pier.

The pier was a huge, fun city, perched on thousands of wooden pilings that marched, like massive log soldiers, for a quarter mile from the boardwalk into the sea. And resting on the pilings, was a most wondrous array of exotic entertainment:

movies with live Vaudeville shows, and big band music, arcades and food stands, a diving bell that dropped beneath the waves, a diving horse that leaped into the waves and even a real Eskimo village.

Back in her mom's room Shelly opens the box she's brought from home and begins showing her mother its contents.

Slowly, as Sarah realizes it's the box from her bedroom, she bursts into a screaming fit.

"You bitch! You fucking bitch! How dare you! What right do you have to steal my treasures? I should call the police. Those are my treasures, Goddammit!"

"Mom, please, I didn't steal it...I just brought it...I thought we could at---

"No bitch is going to tell me what the fuck I want! Get the Goddamn fuck out of my sight!"

It was like a miracle. For fifty cents each, the wonders of the Steel Pier could now be theirs. Morris pushed the dollar bill to the woman sitting in the ticket booth.

By two o'clock they were exhausted, seated on the very end of the Pier, in the Ocean Arena. The water show had just ended with its amazing finale: a spectacular dive from a high platform into the open sea, performed by a scantily clad woman, astride a very large barebacked horse.

Sarah and Morris unwrapped their sandwiches and as the arena stands emptied, happily munched their sandwiches and sipped their Cokes.

Moments later Shelly is standing outside Sarah's suite, hands shaking, and forcing back the tears. Shelly has never before been the focus of her mother's extreme agitation and it scares her. Finally, calm enough to go to the empty dining room, she sits and drinks tea. After a half hour and with some effort, she pulls herself together enough to return, hoping Sarah has had a chance to calm down.

She enters very tentatively. "Hey, Mom, it's me, Shelly."

Sarah is sitting up in bed looking serene and glances up from the magazine she is flipping through.

"Oh, Shelly. When did you get here? You're late. I just finished lunch. I had a wonderful omelet and banana cream pie. I wish you had been here."

With great effort Shelly manages a smile, kisses her mother's cheek, and silently prays her brother will arrive sooner rather than later.

When they left the Pier, Sarah and Morris continued walking, this time South along the beach, down along the edge where the sand was damp and hard-packed. The tide was beginning to rise, and the saltwater foam was reaching higher and higher onto the warm, dry sand. They stopped and took

turns balancing one another so they can remove their shoes and stockings. From that point on, they walked, holding onto their shoes and, once or twice, touching hands.

Friday.

As promised, Penrod has arrived at the "Bird" and is standing in front of an unattended reception desk, impatiently tapping one Gucci clad foot.

Beyond the reception area is a large, nicely decorated lounge. New Age music wafts softly from hidden speakers. A few elderly guests sit in wheelchairs or on sofas. Some alone, others chat with visitors. Several read or watch one of several large screen televisions, listening with Bluetooth headphones so as not to bother others in the area.

Penrod, also thanks to the miracle of Bluetooth, seemingly speaks into the air.

"*...Yes, I'm sure.* I'm not blind. No one is behind the reception desk. Nada. However, there is, you'll be happy to know, a very expensive fresh-flower arrangement on the desk. I guess that's what I'm paying these people for. Hell yeah, come get me.

Sarah and Morris ran in and out of the shallows, dodging the approaching surf, and laughing. For a long stretch the beach was almost empty. Just a lonely bather or two---a man, his suit jacket off and pant legs rolled to his knees, sat on a

blanket, peering through a large pair of binoculars---a few children looked for shells and chased tiny sand crabs.

And then, in the distance, Sarah saw it. They both saw it, stopped and simply stared at the elephant.

Moments later, Shelly appears and embraces her brother.

"You can't imagine how happy I am that you're here, Penny."

Simultaneously, a young girl, obviously the receptionist, returns in a dignified albeit, frantic trot, apologizing all the way.

"I'm *sooo* sorry. Bathroom emergency."

Shelly and Penrod walk slowly to their mother's room, pausing occasionally allowing Shelly to brief her brother, so he will be better prepared for what to expect.

"She's gotten worse. A couple days ago—after we spoke--she started getting very aggressive, yelling at the staff and at me and Pop. And the cursing! Like a drunk sailor. I don't know about you, but I don't think I ever heard Mom curse. Ever? Did you?

"Like, right off hand? No, I can't think of anything that stands out," Penrod says. "Well, actually, she once called me a spoiled little shit."

"That wasn't a curse, just an astute observation," Shelly says, smiles and hugs her brother's arm.

"Now it's non-stop: 'Fuck this and fuck that. Where's my fucking breakfast?' She calls me a fucking bitch. It's embarrassing."

"She still repeats herself?"

"Much more than ever. And her short-term memory is completely shot. Occasionally, she'll come up with little snippets from the past but even those are confused. Like, out of the blue, she said she hates what she thought was my wedding dress, but all the details she hated are about the dress she wore at her wedding. The one in that picture of her and Pop that's in the den. Whatever memory she has left is just a shuffled mishmash of unrelated events and stuff that never happened," Shelly says.

"You think she'll know me?"

"Maybe. Or she may think you're her doctor or her father. Or she might just fake it and pretend she knows who you are. You'll see. But try not to correct her if she says freaky stuff or thinks you're someone else. It just gets her frustrated and she stops talking at all. At some level she knows—or at least, at some point she must have known—her mind was—you know, going… and I'm sure it's been hell for her."

"And Pop? He must be ready to jump out a window?"

"You know Dad, Penny. All he was ever good at was making a nice living, a nice home and a nice life for us. But when it comes to any kind of conflict, illness, difficult family shit? He's useless. He shows up every day, gives her a kiss, sits in the lounger and reads every word of The New York Times. Unless an attendant or one of Mom's doctors comes by, he just reads, takes short naps and goes to the dining room for a coffee every few hours."

Shelly checks her watch and says, "He should be getting here soon."

Sarah had never seen anything like it: a gloriously gigantic elephant, towering over her and looking as big as a building, which in fact, it was.

THE LAST MARBLE

Lucy the Elephant had been built in 1881 as a promotional gimmick to help sell beach-front real estate. In the years that followed, Lucy had been used in various ways—as a hotel, a bar, an office—but its main attraction had always been as a splendid observation tower and magnetic tourist attraction.

Shelly and Penrod enter their mother's room. Truthfully, to call it a room is a misnomer. It's more like a small hotel suite. About the only item that sets it apart from one is an elaborate adjustable hospital bed.

Sarah, even at her advanced age, still possesses remnants of what was once a beautiful woman. Her thick, long, formerly auburn hair is now pure white and has been carefully brushed and braided. In preparation for Penrod's visit, Shelly arranged for the in-house beautician to do her mother's hair, add a touch of makeup, and carefully paint Sarah's nails.

Sarah, always petite is now, at ninety-two, a very small woman. Sitting up in the large hospital bed, she resembles a framed photo surrounded by a mat of white linen bedding.

She's wearing a lovely blue silk bed jacket and a pair of large-framed reading glasses perch on her nose. She slowly thumbs through a magazine, admiring the photographs.

Shelly walks to the bed. "Hi, Mom," and touches her mother's shoulder. Sarah looks up, smiles, and allows the magazine to drop to her lap.

"Mom, look who came from California just to see you.

Penrod approaches the bed, leans over to kiss his mother who recoils, hands raised in alarm.

"Who the fuck are you?"

"Mom, it's me, your son, Penrod."

"Penrod? What kind of God damn name is that? It sounds like what you'd name a dog or a parrot."

"Yeah, I know, Mom," Penrod says, laughing. "I never liked it much either. Sorry, I didn't mean to startle you. You look very nice."

"Sarah squints at her son for a moment, then removes her glasses.

"Oh, of course, you're Penrod, yes. It's these fucking glasses. Your hair is gone. Is that the new style? So, how's school? Do you need me to write you a note? I remember I'm always writing notes to your teachers. Last week you needed one so you could go with the class to the zoo. I write lots of notes to your teachers because you fuck-up so much. Like my brother Malcolm. He would fuck up a lot, too. But he made a bundle in transportation. He was here to see me yesterday."

"Malcolm drove a cab, Mom," then under his breath Penrod added, "He died of a heart attack at my bar mitzvah."

Sarah points at her son and wags her finger. "I know you now. You're Penrod, right?

"Right."

"You're the one who gave me a sponge bath yesterday.

The rhythmic sound of crashing waves pounded in her ears and the clean, briny smell of salt air filled her nostrils.

Sarah stood, arms wide in a child-like gesture of pure happiness, her white patent-leather shoes clutched in one hand.

Her starched white sailor dress looking crisp and bright in the strong glare of mid-day sun. Sarah's thick hair—its color the deepest shade of rust—fell to her shoulders and moved easily like a shiny wave in the strong, salted breeze.

Just then Sarah's husband walks into the room. The folded newspaper is under his arm. He kisses Shelly, and when he spots his son, Penrod, they embrace. J.D. hugs Penrod and kisses him on both cheeks.

J.D. then steps to the bed and leans down to kiss Sarah. She pushes him away.

"Don't come near me, you pervert. Clean the room! That's your fucking job and then get the fuck out of here."

J.D. doesn't seem fazed and grabs Penrod's arm. "Boy, do I miss you, kiddo. Really miss you. If Mom wasn't—you know—anyway, if she was okay, I'd fly out to see you a lot. Just one of the benefits of being retired."

Penny and his dad move away and out of earshot of the women.

"Clearly, Mom's not doing so good, Pop. How are you holding up?" Penrod says, softly.

"Me? Don't you worry. I'm fine. A bit lonely, to tell the truth. I come here every day and read. You can't talk to her. I don't mean I can't actually speak to her, but nothing of any substance comes back. You just saw. She doesn't recognize me---or anyone, for that matter. She's not gone, but she is…*gone*. If you know what I mean?"

She watched as the ocean rose in huge blue-green swells that rolled into waves, smashing against the shoreline and reaching out with thick foam fingers stretching toward dry sand. Hundreds of snow-white gulls seemed to fill the sky. Wings extended, they hung motionless on strong, invisible currents of air—occasionally folding back their wings to dive for food from the sea.

The packed sand in the shade beneath the elephant felt damp and cool to Sarah's bare feet. Never in all her life had she felt this happy, this free and this alive.

The next morning, Saturday, Shelly makes breakfast for Penny and J.D. Then they discussed Sarah, a subject that literally sucks the oxygen out of the air. On one point they are in agreement: Sarah would never return to any kind of reasonable life. In fact, it's probably time to move her out of the suite and into the Bird's Total-Care facility. The remaining options have come down to a question of how to keep Sarah comfortable until the ultimate end. She has mostly stopped eating. She picks at the food trays that are placed in front of her three times each day. And although she is losing her ability to use the silverware, she refuses to be fed by anyone. She is literally shrinking, little-by-little each day.

Once Penrod learns there is WiFi in the Bird's visitor's lounge, he spends endless hours on Zoom calls. Between calls, he sits with Shelly and J.D. watching Sarah. She ate almost nothing and, since Penny arrived, spoke less and less—including the cursing.

It is afternoon. J.D. is engrossed in the newspaper's Op-ed page and responding to the content under his breath. Penny is back from a marathon Zoom meeting with "the coast" and Shelly sits in a chair next to the bed rummaging through Sarah's box of treasures.

"Would you like to go up inside," Morris asked? "I think there's a charge... I...have...some money left," he added with more than a touch of hesitation. Before answering, Sarah took a few steps out from where they were standing, and shielding her eyes from the sun, gazed up at the sixty-five-foot-high structure.

Sarah desperately wanted to go to the very top, to stand in the Howdah on Lucy's back and see the panoramic views. She also feared that the admission charge, on top of what Morris had already spent at The Steel Pier, would be more than he could afford and didn't want to embarrass him, especially since, as Ida had pointed out, Morris Blinderman was most likely poor.

Shelly pulls a few pictures from the box and shows them to Sarah.

"Mom, do you know who this is?" Sarah looks at the picture of herself when she was in her teens. No response. "That's you when you were a young girl. Sarah stares at the picture for several moments then declares in a faint whisper, "I was a young girl."

Several more pictures are shown to Sarah. Nothing is recognizable, nor does Shelly expect them to be. Sarah has not just lost her memory, it's as if her mind is a chalk board that's been erased and washed clean.

"Shelly, sweetheart, you're just making yourself crazy," J.D. said, lowering his ubiquitous newspaper. "Can't you see she's gone. You can show her that stuff 'til you're blue in the face. But her marbles are gone. Nothing is left in there.

Morris Blinderman watched Sarah as she walked out from the cool shade under Lucy the Elephant. There was no doubt in his mind that Sarah was the most beautiful girl that he'd ever seen. On one hand, he knew he had fallen deeply in love with her. In love, in that special way reserved exclusively for teen-age boys. On the other hand, he knew he had no money left and was filled with the fear that Sarah would want to explore the interior of Lucy the Elephant. He thought he would die before he disappointed her.

Shelly is frustrated, along with a growing resentment toward her father, given his passive resignation toward Sarah's condition. Shelly will not stop trying. She keeps showing her mother picture after picture. Not even a glimmer of recognition is returned. A picture of the dog they had growing up. Her name was Lox because she had a sort of reddish color coat and Sarah loved that mutt. Nothing. Her best friend and Ma Jong partner, with whom she spoke several times every day. Sarah could have been looking at a blank piece of paper.

And J.D. kept injecting his negative point of view. "Shelly, please, you're just torturing yourself. She's lost her marbles. Let her be. Penny, you tell her. She won't listen to me.

Young Morris Blinderman's deep thoughts were interrupted by Sarah's voice, close enough to his ear to feel her breath. "Let's stay here, in the shade, Morris. We don't have to go to the top. Besides, I really don't like high places."

Without thinking – almost as if he were outside of his own body – Morris closed the short distance between them and kissed Sarah. She did not pull away. She dropped her shoes and they landed on the cool sand next to his.

Shelly gave up. "Fuck it," she exclaimed and left the box on Sarah's bed and went into the hall. A smoking room was a few doors down and Shelly went in and bummed a cigarette from an intern on her break. It will soon be over, Shelly thought. And then she felt guilty about thinking it.

She couldn't cry any more. No tears were left. She had devoted the past twelve months of her life to caring for her mother. She had to get back to some sort of life for herself. She stubbed out the cigarette and went back to her mother's room.

J.D. was deep into his New York Times. Penrod was texting on his iPhone. And Sarah was holding a worn post card. A small tear on one side was Scotch taped and the address and message had age-faded long ago. She studied the tattered piece of cardboard—held it between her slender, immaculately manicured thumb and forefinger. A smile formed on her lips.

The front of the card showed the muted tones of a hand-colored photo of an elephant. Under the picture was a printed legend that read, 'Lucy, The Pachyderm Palace.'

It was a long albeit rather chaste kiss. A first kiss for both of them. Possibly a kiss to be remembered.

"Someday, I will marry you," Morris blurted out, close to tears, with emotion, and filled with sweet adolescent joy. "I swear Sarah, you will be my wife."

The next morning, as scheduled, Morris Blinderman left Atlantic City. He and Sarah never again spoke, never exchanged correspondence, or ever again laid eyes on each other.

"This is the elephant—she was called Lucy," Sarah said, pronouncing each word in a distinctly clear voice.

J.D. looked up from his paper. Penrod stopped and turned toward his mother. Shelly stood, her mouth open in surprise.

"Yes. The elephant. I was there with Morris Blinderman, when I was fifteen. We went to The Steel Pier, and we ate cream cheese and jelly sandwiches—we sat and watched when the horse dove into the water. We had such a good time. I wore a new, white sailor dress and a blue bow in my hair. Morris kissed me. He said he loved me."

Then, instead of handing the card back to Penrod, she pressed it to her frail bosom, smiling, her eyes focused on a thought very, very far away.

"I never saw him again."

No one said a word. Somehow, from the rubble of his mother's destroyed memory, a sole survivor had miraculously been found alive.

THE LAST MARBLE

Buried for almost eight decades, it was miraculously still breathing, despite the irreparable damage that so totally surrounded it.

Sarah, it seemed, had lost all her marbles. Save for one.

STORY III
THE BIG KISS

THE BIG KISS

As newly hired, untrained employees, Ashby LaRoy and Carol Breslin are assigned jobs bagging customer's purchases as the check-out cashier scans each item—and every hour or so, corralling the discarded shopping carts left helter-skelter all over the parking lot.

Ashby and Carol—CB to those who know her—quickly become best friends. And, after several months of working and hanging out together, decide to pool their individual rent money, get a larger apartment, and move in together. They easily find a small, yet lovely, two bedroom, two bath garden level rental, that's walking distance from both work, as well as the vibrant Pomona city center.

After almost five years climbing Food Festival Market's corporate ladder, Ashby is now head cashier and CB is the assistant manager—both women working the day shift.

Ashby and CB are in their mid-fifties, divorced and, due to any number of circumstances—age, social standing, education, etc.—have decided their chances of finding a decent, reliable boyfriend, let alone a serviceable husband, are slightly less likely than turning water into wine.

So, with the concept of 'romance' removed from their vocabulary of possibilities, they find enjoyment in each other's company—more like sisters than just friends. They shop and cook and even vacation together. When they're not working or enjoying the benefits of living in a cultural city like Pomona, they enjoy 'bingeing' British TV series and watching old American movies on their sixty-inch Sony smart TV.

They also enjoy consuming lots of red wine. And, thanks to a friendly Food Festival butcher, are blessed with a steady supply of excellent cannabis— the latter smoked on weekends only—since as members of Food Festival's middle-management they feel obligated to set a good example.

The rain started early Saturday morning and continued all day. It's evening now and the rain hasn't let up. Loud thunder rolls continuously, often punctuated by ear-splitting cracks of blindingly bright lightning.

Thanks to a generous 'gift' from the very same friendly Food Festival butcher, CB and Ashby devoured four delicious double cut lamb chops, washed down with a bottle of 1990 Jordon California Cabernet. They figure with the meat and the grapes, they have most of the food groups covered.

Dishes done and kitchen clean, Ashby and CB are relaxing in their living room—warm and snug in their PJs, robes, and matching bunny slippers.

They are sated and a bit smashed and pass a hefty 'doobie' of excellent weed back and forth.

CB is sprawled across the large sectional sofa, her head in the grip of one of those soft, 'U' shape airline pillows. Ashby is reclining nearby on a large red beanbag—it's about the only seating she's found that can ease her back pain, especially after a long day on her feet at the market.

They are engrossed watching the last few minutes of one of their old Thin Man movies.

The six film collection of Thin Man films starring Myrna Loy and William Powel was a Christmas gift from CB to Ashby. They love the series and watch it at least once a month. They know every word of dialogue by heart and often speak the lines out loud, along with the actors.

Weather aside, they are snug, dry, well-fed, and, for the umpteenth time, enjoying the classic old movie series.

The cozy living room is furnished nicely with a traditional-style upholstered sofa and two large matching armchairs. Several colorful pillows are scattered about. A large coffee table fashioned from a steel workbench of some sort stands between the chairs. A few older restored pieces "rescued" from Pomona's Antique Row, provide a warm, "lived-in" look. Ashby and CB purchased a large Persian carpet at a garage sale and carried it back to their apartment on their shoulders, rolled up like it might contain a dead body. Once laid, it served to pull the whole room together.

The apartment blooms with lots of flourishing plants thanks to CB's green thumb. The pungent aroma of eucalyptus hangs in the air and is quite pleasant.

CB stands up and poses in a full-body stretch. "I need a tall glass of cold water," she says. "My tongue is so dry it's sticking to the roof of my mouth. Do you wa…wan…

Suddenly, and without warning, CB is cut off by an ear-splitting, violent CRACK! And the living room explodes with brilliant, blinding light.

Sharp, jagged Sparks, dance erratically while dozens of tiny flames, scamper over lamps, walls, furniture and up and across CB's body as she stands, frozen, arms spread and mouth agape in mid-stretch in front of the couch. Her body is shaking as if in a seizure, but she's unable to move. The sparks and tiny flames dance and bounce from her and then converge onto Ashby, wrapping around and through her body. Sparks of light and fire fly from her mouth, ears and eyes. One shaking hand pleadingly reaches out toward CB, the other grabs a fistful of the beanbag in a powerful, vice-like grip.

The intensity of the light and tiny dancing flames slowly subside, funnel through the TV and run up the walls and then, in an instant, are gone.

The sharp smell of ozone remains and triggers in Ashby a memory of the toy trains her father would set up every Christmas. With the metal tracks assembled and the transformer plugged into the wall socket, Ashby would experience this same acrid electric smell.

As if released by a giant hand, CB drops back onto the couch and lays, frozen, her thick hair standing out—like a-finger-in-a-socket cartoon. She's too stunned and stoned to react even though she is scared half-to-death.

In what seems like forever—CB finally musters a modicum of control and leaps the distance from couch to beanbag and wraps her arms around Ashby. Both women are weeping as a rolling tsunami of sound follows the lightning and slowly, reluctantly departs.

"Wha…wa…what the fuck!" CB manages to say.

Ashby is speechless and just sits, dazed, allowing CB to hold her.

Finally, "Holy Christ, I thought that shit only happened on golf courses," CB says. "You lit up like a fucking Christmas tree. I swear I thought you were dead. I'm talking Bride of Frankenstein shit."

CB runs her hands all over her body making sure nothing is missing or damaged. She feels the familiar texture of her chenille bathrobe, then says, "Shit!"

"What? Are you hurt?" Ashby says, concerned.

"No, but it burned my robe! CB said. "That's how close that fucker came to me. Imagine if I wasn't wearing it, I might look like the burnt end of a match right now."

"The lights, the TV," Ashby said, just realizing they are all out. "Circuit breakers. I have to…you know. I think they're in the kitchen. The lights never went out before."

"You okay to walk around? Maybe you should lie down or something," CB says.

Ashby stands a bit unsteadily, "I think I'm okay. Just feel a little fried."

"Fried. That's funny. Me, I feel like burnt toast," CB mutters, using her pajama sleeve to wipe the tears from her cheeks. "I feel like a piece of burnt toast.

"Plus, my robe is ruined. That's the second one I've fucked up. You remember the one I ripped on the fridge handle?"

"The yellow one," Ashby yells from the kitchen as she rummages in a drawer for the flashlight.

"Yeah, Dammit, that one."

Ashby finds the fuse box inside one of the cabinets and behind a half-dozen assorted brands of breakfast cereal. She flips the long row of switches. The television blare and sudden glare of lights snap to life simultaneously, momentarily scaring the crap out of both women.

Back again on the couch with CB, Ashby reaches over, pulls CB's robe toward her, and myopically checks the damage. Sure enough, it has a hole burned right into it. And she can even smell the lingering electric odor of lightning.

"You're right, CB, it certainly is fucked up. Tell you what," Ashby giggles, trying her best to get them both in a better mood after their near-death experience. "Don't cry over spilt chenille. I'll kiss it and make it better." And she pulls a handful of the wine-colored chenille to her mouth.

The robe smells of electricity and CB's Arid Extra Dry Deodorant. And CB stops crying and laughs as Ashby smooches the rough material.

"Appreciate the gesture, girl, but I don't think it's going to do diddly squat for a burned hole."

"What a night. I'm still shaking," CB said. "I'm blasted. Need sleep. Whoever gets up first makes the coffee. G'night, Ash."

CB just about makes it to her bedroom and wrapped in her burnt chenille robe, falls instantly into a deep, snoring coma.

Ashby stays awake drinks a beer while watching the end of The Thin Man movie. Then she presses the remote, shrinking its image to a pencil point of light before going black.

Lacking the energy to leave her comfortable beanbag, Ashby falls quickly into a sound sleep in spite of—or possibly due to— the continuing low grumble of thunder.

THE BIG KISS

Ashby is friendly with a neighbor, Lorna Major, another divorced lady. Lorna has a five-year-old daughter, Pinky, who Ashby occasionally baby-sits.

Little Pinky Major is a cute kid. Well-behaved and easy to care for. One Sunday afternoon Ashby is minding Pinky for Lorna and takes her to a nearby playground. To many locals it's known as The Daddy Park, so named because so many divorced fathers bring their kids there on their custody days. As a logical consequence, divorced women also show up with their kids. While the children play, the adults check out other people's discarded spouses. It is not unlike rummaging through a flea market, searching for overlooked, albeit slightly worn human treasures.

Ashby enjoys the warm California sun, relaxing on a bench as it makes love to her face. Suddenly, through the laughter and shouting, she hears Pinky crying. Mothers have that kind of built-in radar and even though Ashby's own kid is grown, she never lost the skill. Like not forgetting how to change a diaper or make a square knot.

"Waaaaaaaaaaaaaa," little Pinky Major bawls, tears and snot making their way toward her chin, her plump little legs propel her toward Ashby.

"There, there, baby…don't cry…" Ashby cooed, hugging the child to her ample bosom.

"Waaaaaaaaaaaaaa!" Pinky blubbers, the way little kids are wont to do. "Make it better aunt Athbee. Tith it, Tith it! And make it better. Waaaaaaaaaaaaaaa."

"Oh, kiss it," Ashby says, finally translating Pinky's cute toddler lisp. Ashby uses a sanitary wipe dug from her handbag to clean the wound. She then plants a smackeroo on the scraped elbow that Pinky pushes up toward Ashby, her little fist in the air—a tiny power-to-the-people gesture.

Minutes later a laughing Pinky Major is back at play, her scrape forgotten, while Ashby returns to her current love, the sun.

After work, a few nights later, CB heads home while Ashby detours to pick up Chinese for their dinner.

Thirty minutes later, Ashby arrives home. Her left arm circles the large paper bag containing their dinner, the right hand gropes her pocket for her key. Before she can use it, the door bursts open and she's confronted by CB, visibly agitated.

"Remember my robe," CB demands?

Ashby gives CB a blank look and asks, "Would you like to give me a hand? Please. Getting Won Ton soup out of a Persian rug is a bitch."

"You know, that night. When I was almost electrocuted?"

"You mean when we were BOTH almost electrocuted. Remember? Shit, who could forget it?"

CB takes the bag from Ashby, walks to the kitchen, drops the bag of food on the kitchen counter and goes to her bedroom. She's back seconds later with a chenille robe over her arm.

"This! Do you remember this?

Ashby looked at the robe. She nodded. "Yeah, it's your old chenille robe. Your point is?"

"Look at the right side—that's where it burned—look at it!" CB demanded with an edgy voice.

Ashby took it, turning the cloth slowly in her hands. Who could forget, especially with the damn Arid Extra Dry smell pushing the memory into her nose and straight to her brain? Her fingers part the chenille nap, searching for the lightning damage.

"Yeah, okay, what am I'm looking at?"

"You know damned well," CB said.

"Christ, CB! Give me a hint—what the fuck am I looking for?"

CB's face was flushed as she leaned in close to Ashby. "You kissed it, remember? To make it better. Remember?"

Ashby stands, her eyes fixed on the robe in her hand.

"For crying out loud, CB—don't be an asshole. I was just stoned and still in shock about us both almost getting zapped to death. So, I was joking around. Obviously, you bought a new robe. I'll pay for the damned thing if it's such a problem. It's just a fucking bathrobe. So, what's the big deal?" Ashby says.

"What's the big deal? I'll tell you what's the big fucking deal. Look," CB said, grabbing a handful of Chenille and pushing it close to Ashby's face. "That's the big deal! I didn't buy a new robe. It's the same damned robe that was burned by the lightning." CB was shaking as she spoke and, Ashby, for the first time, felt a shiver in her back to her butt, and her whole body reflexed, like a horse's rump when it shucks-off a fly.

Ashby examined the robe again, this time, methodically, going from sleeve to sleeve and front to back. "Okay, so you took it to that dry cleaner on main street where they do the 'magic weaving,' thing, right?" Ashby exclaimed, yet asked, at the same time.

CB snatched back the robe. She held it by the collar and gave it a shake then folded it across her free arm. She was standing with her back to the TV and the light turned her thin nightgown translucent.

Quietly, very quietly CB began, her voice quivering as she spoke. "I…did not…touch…this robe. Never put a needle to it, never had it magic-woven…nothing, I swear. That…that burn hole," she continues, her excitement level rising. "It wasn't just some pulled-open seam, either. It was an honest-to-God hole! All raggedy and scorched. With that kind of fucking damage all you can do is stitch the crap out of it with a ton of heavy thread and no matter what you do, it puckers and looks like crap! If it was mended like that, a blind person could see it."

Ashby instinctively takes a step toward CB and puts her arms around her, comforting her as one would a child.

"Hey, come on, kiddo, pull yourself together. It's just a robe. There's a perfectly reasonable explanation for this. Don't get so upset."

"Sure there is," CB shouts, her voice driven with alarm. "I know damn well what the explanation is. I'm having a nervous break job!"

"Down. A break down," Ashby reflexively corrects her, then wishes she hadn't.

"It finally hit me, Ash! I've gone mental! I'm ready for the funny farm. Maybe it's the weed we've been smoking? Or God punishing us for taking those lamb chops and stuff from the market."

"You're not crazy," Ashby says in a soothing but firm way as she tilts CB forward, so she has to put her foot out for balance and by so doing, they walk, step-by-step toward the sofa.

"I'm frigging bat shit," CB mumbles as Ashby holds her and rocks her.

"Look, honey," Ashby says, "I was there, too. We both saw the rip. I remember the hole. It was a mother of a mess—like you said—jagged and all. So you're not crazy. It's simple. The damn robe was badly damaged and now—well, now—the—robe—is, you know. Not."

Then Ashby stops, suddenly struck by the realization of what she said, yet not knowing exactly what the next words should be.

Uh, so, and now—so, and now—the—robe—is—not. Damaged? And Ashby's voice trails off like the slow dying sound of an echo.

It takes a moment for CB to digest what Ashby is saying.

"Shit," CB says. "Of course, I'm not crazy. The robe was, you know—and now—and now—and now—Oh HELL, Ashby, we're BOTH crazy."

Ashby sits on the bed with CB until she finally falls into a fitful sleep. Then goes to the kitchen, pours herself an inch of Jack Daniels and takes it, along with the bottle, into the living room and wriggles into a comfortable position on her beanbag.

She needs time to think. But given the circumstances, Ashby isn't quite sure what to think about.

It's a hot, humid evening and Lorna Major is sitting on the stoop outside of her apartment having a smoke and trying to catch a breeze when Ashby returns from work.

"Hey, Ash," Lorna says.

"Hey, Lorna. By the way, how's Pinky's elbow?"

"Pinky's elbow?" she says Then her face smiles. Oh, right, Pinky says she hurt it in the park. But it looked okay to me…not a mark. She says you kissed it and made it better. I'm impressed. That's one hell of a smooch you got there, honey," Lorna says, blowing a plume of tobacco carcinogens into the humid night air. "No scab. Not even a red mark. Nothing."

"Uh, that's good. I was concerned. Well, goodnight," Ashby says, and heads to her apartment, feeling a vague soupçon of dread.

At 3 a.m. Ashby snaps out of a sound sleep, wide-awake in the nanosecond it takes for her eyes to open.

That's just plain madness!

For the next ten minutes Ashby sits on the edge of the bed smoking a cigarette, trying to decide her next move. Finally, she marches purposefully to the closet, flings it open, reaches in to snare an attractive green jersey dress. She pulls it out with such violence that it snaps its plastic hanger. Ashby grasps the garment firmly in both hands and with one burst of effort, rips it about six-inches down the front.

Ashby returns to bed where, crouches down in the dark, she hugs the damaged dress tightly to her naked body. The tiny interior light from the open closet throws long shadows across the walls. She feels delirious, as if in a dream, but she knows she isn't dreaming. She can feel the softness of the green jersey on her naked stomach and between her legs. She licks her lips nervously.

"I must be unhinged," she murmurs under her breath. "I've just ruined a $200 dress!"

Ashby licks her lips and then, slowly, sensuously, begins running her lips over the uneven edges of the ripped material—her soft tongue pushing at the loose threads. For the next few minutes, she licks and kisses and rubs the dress. It is strangely exciting and, much to her astonishment and embarrassment, she experiences a powerful orgasm.

"My god!" she says, finally catching her breath, "I just fucked my dress!" Then, humiliated, she walks to the bathroom to wash, leaving the dress on the floor at the foot of the bed.

By morning she's forgotten the incident of the night before. However, as she rolls out of bed and sees the dress on the floor, the memory of her stupid experiment instantly returns. She pads, naked, to the bathroom to shower. Afterward, since it's her day off, she pulls on a pair of jeans and her favorite sweatshirt and grabs the green dress she sexually violated, intending to toss it into the trash. A perfectly nice, and rather expensive dress wasted.

But as soon as she touches it, without even looking, she knows. And when she finally gets the courage to look, there is not a rip, not a blemish, not a mark. The dress is as good as new.

No longer is there any doubt.

First, CB's robe.

Then, little Pinky's elbow.

And now my own dress.

Somehow, for whatever reason, Ashby LaRoy had been granted The Power to Heal. With her mouth!

Melvin 'Dimples' Napoli has just married the exquisitely beautiful Flora Promissori, Don Promissori's only child. And solely by virtue of that coupling, Dimples—a low-level soldier in the rival Napoli family—has been allowed into the Promissori family.

The wedding dinner is a brilliant display of vulgarity. The harried wait staff serve more courses than it takes to earn a degree from Harvard.

All evening, two of the Don Promissori's overweight flunkies—both stuffed into tight tuxedos—shadow the bride, bearing satin bags, the size of pillowcases, filling with fat envelopes, each containing gifts from Promissoris, Napolis and guests, and each envelope containing more than good wishes.

Since their first meeting Don Promissori made it clear to Dimples, that his daughter's virginity was inviolate, at least until her wedding night.

So, Dimples has spent many celibate months in agonizing anticipation. Now, finally on the wedding day, he is locked and loaded and ready to give Flora his best sexual shot. At an appropriate moment, the newlyweds steal away to a baronial suite on the top floor of the hotel, there to consummate their union.

Flora uses one bathroom to prepare while Dimples uses the second bathroom. After some time, he slips into the conjugal bed, naked, scented, and glowing pink from a long, hot shower.

A naked Flora is waiting in semi-darkness on the soccer-pitch-size bed. Her thick auburn hair fans across the large satin covered pillow. A satin sheet traces every curve of her breathtaking body.

Dimples slides under the covers and presses his well-muscled body along her entire length. She is immediately aroused. Then, drawing from his sophomoric lexicon of sexual knowledge, he blows into her ear as one might try to clear a clogged gas line. He mistakes Flora's violent response, for passion, and throws himself across her body.

He then proceeds to "do it" five times. Unfortunately for the bride, five times to Dimples means five spastic hip thrusts, which barely moisten Flora's carnal desires, let alone anything else.

Dimples is sleeping soundly even before Flora has fully recovered from the unexpected ear blowing.

Their sex life drifts downhill from there.

Each learn to compensate. Flora first tried to educate Dimples, but he is no better at mastering sexual technique than he was trying to learn long division back in grade school.

Next, Flora seeks satisfaction from various electrical appliances—turning then, eventually, to a series of live male appliances.

Dimples compensates by burrowing himself in his work for Don Promissori and playing the horses.

Life is good for Dimples, save for his nagging history of sexual performance issues. This will soon change.

One Thursday at midnight, by mere coincidence, CB and

Dimples are both at the Food Festival. CB is there 'covering' the night shift for the other assistant manager, who is attending a wedding. Dimples, to collect the weekly envelope containing protection money for Don Promissori, from the owners of the Food Festival.

On the night CB bumped into Dimples he was feeling a bit lonely. So, on a whim, he asked her to join him for coffee. The coffee led to dinner a few nights later and that, to a room at the Hollywood Roosevelt hotel.

The Thursday's coffee and hotel didn't last very long.

Dimples' sexual proficiency was no better with CB than it had been with Flora and, to avoid him, CB stayed away from the Food Festival and only worked day shifts.

A few weeks later Dimples found CB at a bookstore in Westwood and attempted to reignite their tepid weekly affair.

CB, convinced by her troubling lack of self-esteem, assumes Dimples' performance problem is, at least partially her fault. She decides to introduce him to her friend and apartment mate, Ashby, thinking she will have better luck with the guy.

It's not as if Dimples is a total washout. He's good looking, about six foot and built like a middle linebacker. He dresses well and has a great car. And he would die before he'd ask a date to split a dinner check.

It's just that Dimples is a little slow. Not the thickest slice in the loaf of life.

So, CB arranges the introduction, and a week later Dimples dutifully appears on Ashby's doorstep.

"You know how to make an egg cream?" he asks, as he enters her apartment. "I love 'em ...wit' Scotch."

And he has a good sense of humor.

Dimples immediately feels comfortable with Ashby. More

relaxed. For some reason, he sees her more like a buddy, and feels somehow released from any pressure to perform sexually.

Dimples' release from performance pressure lasts up to their third date, when, after polishing off several martinis, Ashby gives Dimples a spectacular blowjob.

A few days later, Dimples, the 'buddy' fantasy long gone, is back at Ashby's place, horny and hoping for an encore.

In his initial oral encounter with Ashby, Dimples experienced some difficulty fulfilling his end of the bargain. This time the difference is notable, in the extreme. A-stud-horse-in-heat analogy gallops to mind. He is a man possessed. It's as if he is a teenager again, only this time with plenty of pocket money and, for what it's worth, a damned nice car.

To say Dimples is grateful for his mysterious sexual metamorphosis—from the limp to the laudable—would be an understatement.

As for his sex-starved wife, Dimples' cure is a godsend and, in due course, she is reduced to a quivering mass of sexual satisfaction at the hands of her husband's 'born again' libido.

Ashby strongly suspects that Dimples, like her green dress and Pinky's elbow, has been "repaired" by her powers. Nevertheless, she keeps the information to herself.

Soon after his Lourdes-like healing, Dimples tracks down CB at the Food Festival and thanks her profusely for making the introduction to Ashby. He then proceeds to describe in detail all that has sexually transpired.

Trying to summarize, Dimples finally comes up with: "She's one amazing broad," and crosses himself. "She is damned good for me. And things with Flora have never been better."

"Sounds like you're a walking dildo now, Dimples," CB says.

"Ash has that effect—not sure what to call it—it's this thing—this kind of power, you know."

Dimples just looks puzzled, brow creased, head cocked, not understanding what kind of power CB is talking about.

Translating the look, CB says, "There has been certain—let's call it strange incidents…" and her voice trails off.

Dimples, continues to stare, his mind moving at turtle-like speed, trying to make sense of what CB is inferring.

"Do you understand what I'm saying, Dimples?" CB pauses for a beat or two.

No, of course, you don't understand, do you?

So, as Dimples and CB push an empty cart through the Food Festival aisles, she relates in detail the story of Ashby's mysterious powers. Dimples trails along, hanging on CB's every word, the Food Festival's envelope stuffed with protection money clutched in his beefy, manicured fist.

Dimples' boss, Don Promissori had been very sexually active, back in the day. Capable, it was said, of satisfying multiple women in a single evening. Although small in stature, his member was the stuff of legend.

But that was then. Now, Don Promissori—old and shriveled—can only relive past sexual glories in his fast-fading memory. This makes the Don very cranky and as a consequence, those around him suffer. Not the least of which is Dimples, the body guard Don Promissori always wished he had.

Therefore, it made sense that three nights after CB spilled the beans about Ashby's mysterious powers, Dimples arrives to present

Ashby with a logical, albeit wacky proposition.

After some superficial chit-chat, Dimples suggests he has a plan for Ashby to earn a very large amount of money.

"It would be yours, in hard cash and tax-free if you could see your way clear to, like, do your magic on my esteemed father-in-law."

Ashby is furious. "First of all, Dimples, CB has no right to talk about that—to you or anybody else. If she thinks I'm some sort of freak she can pimp out, she's gone mental.

"And as far as your asshole boss, you dumb dago putz! I'd rather go down on the Titanic than on Don Promissori," Ashby screams before Dimples can clamp his hand over her mouth.

"Trust me Ashby," Dimples whispered into her ear, his beefy hand smothering her mouth, "this attitude you're displaying toward a boat-load of cash don't seem collegial, ya know, so how's about you give it another think or I will be forced to bend your knees opposite what nature intended."

The effectiveness of Dimples' simple plea, honed from years of collecting protection money, worked its magic, and a terrified Ashby is forced to think twice about mounting any further arguments.

And so, one evening, the following week, Dimples arrives with a skeptical Don Promissori in tow. Later, as the two men are leaving, Don Promissori thanks Ashby, as Dimples hands her a thick envelope containing many crisp, hundred-dollar bills.

By the next day, after a good night's sleep, a hot shower, and an enjoyable shopping spree on Rodeo Drive, Ashby begins to believe the session with Don Promissori just might have been worth it.

She even makes up with CB and forgives her for having a mouth as big as her heart.

As if responding to her rationalized and cash-fueled change of attitude, and considering the Don's miraculous regression back to his over-sexed youth, Dimples shows up with a second E-D-challenged mobster carrying more crisp Franklins. And, after that, the men and the money pours in like lava flowing from a volcano.

Two months pass quickly.

Dimples is sitting in Ashby's bedroom sipping a Scotch-laced egg cream, as he ponders the gold mine, he's stumbled across. Ashby, seated in an attractive dressing gown, stops shaving a corn on the outer edge of her right foot, and says, "Dimples, you're out of your mind! No way I'm leaving Los Angeles."

"Hey, don't give me any crap. You are doing right okay, no?"

It was true. Ashby had indeed been doing right okay. In fact, she already had a growing bundle in the bank and business was getting brisker. There seemed to be no end to the parade of limp male members, and word-of-mouth, about her mouth, was spreading.

"Okay, look, I'm first to admit things have been great, but what's this about moving out of L.A., for Christ's sake? I'm lonely enough here. The only people I see are CB and you and mostly, the bottom half of my clients."

Dimples put his drink down on the bedside table and attempts to collect his thoughts. Not an easy task in such a leaky container.

"Ash, you have done more for sex—to help guys with sex problems—than—than—" Dimples's mental wheels spun in the soft mush of his mind groping for an analogy, "—than Howard and Johnson!

"Masters, Dimples. Masters and Johnson,"

"Yeah. Whatever," Dimples says. "Look, I talked it over with the Don and we think it would be best if you and CB got out of town. It's too dangerous here. What if the newspapers get wind of this?

"You think it's less dangerous in New York or Chicago?"

Dimples mumbles, "We think you should relocate in...."

The rest of what Dimples said is illegible."

"What'd you say?"

"France," Dimples says, weakly. "We think you and CB should leave the country," he says with more confidence.

"Are you out of your fucking mind? What you think this is, Blowjobs Without Borders? And we have lives here. Jobs. Friends."

Dimples frowns, "Jobs? You both work in a fucking supermarket. And as long as I've known you, I've never seen or met any so-called friends of yours or CB's."

At least, over there, living in a high-class hotel—hell, your gift can stay hush-hush. Eyes only, you know? Like a secret agent in the CIO."

"A, it's the CIA. The CIO is a union, asshole."

"Ash, ya gotta trust me on this. France is class. You ever seen the Riviera? It's stinking with class."

"And I guess you been there, Dimples?" Ashby said sarcastically.

"As a matter of fact, wise ass, I have. Once. Had to go make a big collection from a guy in Nice. That's a place on the Riviera. The broads there wear bikinis with no tops."

"It's real nice, huh?" Ashby said, slightly impressed.

"Nice? Shit, that town is better than—" Dimples' mind struggles for a benchmark that will help Ashby visualize Nice, "—it's better than Atlantic City!"

Ashby walks into the kitchen, fills a glass with water and stands by the sink sipping the water and thinking. She finally returns to Dimples.

"I need to talk it over with CB. Gimme a day or two, okay?"

It takes about two-minutes for Ashby and CB to grab onto the lucrative and all-expenses-paid-offer. Within a week they quit their jobs at the Food Festival and sublet their apartment.

Two weeks later, an excited and slightly skeptical Ashby and CB are in Nice, France, living in a luxury suite at the swank Negresco Hotel. As Dimples predicted, Ashby's distance from Los Angeles creates an immediate aura of efficacy, which, as he also predicted, would justify much higher rates for the miracles she performs.

Ashby and CB transition easily and quickly into their new life. Both lose a little weight, turn brown as berries from hours of beach time, and even buy matching string bikinis. After their first trip to the beach in the bikinis, they revert to once-piece bathing costumes.

Then there is their leased chocolate brown Porsche 911 in the garage. Both catch up on a raft of reading, people-watching, and many umbrella-drinks on the terrace of the historic French hotel.

The financial arrangements are quite simple. The hotel bills, room, and food are paid directly by Dimples from America. In addition, after each service rendered, Dimples wire transfers large sums into Ashby's personal account.

Dimples always plays it straight with Ashby. She gets half of the gross collected from the client and pays her expenses out of his half.

And so, for the first time in a long while, Ashby is happy.

Every couple of weeks—sometime every week and, on occasion, several times a week—Dimples brings or sends "friends" —they come in all shapes, sizes and ages, each suffering from the same problem.

"Anozer limp noodle, eh, Dimples?" Ashby would say, effecting a recently acquired French inflection.

"Just use your power, baby," Dimples would say on cue. "I'm gonna make you rich."

Within hours after enjoying a treatment from Ashby, her client would invariably be as stiff as a broom handle. Some headed straight back to America. Many roamed the female-filled topless beaches, wild-eyed and clutching a towel or robe over their tumescent members.

Word of her success spread beyond the "family," and she began to attract clientele from among the great and near great. Some who visited were politicians, financiers—movers and shakers—many were movie and TV actors whom she recognized from magazines, newspapers. She healed them all. To Ashby, from the waist down, all men were equal.

Ashby feels fulfilled and proud of doing something fine for mankind. Not unlike Albert Schweitzer treating the lepers or Ray Kroc inventing the Big Mac.

At times, usually in the evenings after a few martinis, she jokes to CB about being named a Saint. Our Lady Of The Crotch? Something like that.

As for her power, it seemed to be growing and evolving with use. Obviously she mended all her own clothing. Once, on an afternoon spent in Monte Carlo, Ashby's Porsche was badly scratched. For the next few nights, in the cool, quiet of the Negresco Hotel's underground garage, she worked over the ugly gouge that marred the chocolate brown fender. By week's end, the fender was like new, the paint color perfect.

It is a warm August evening when Dimples calls from America.

"Ash, baby," Dimples voice booms, clear as glass, across the Atlantic, "I got a very special one for you, okay?"

"I'm fine, Dimples. Thanks for asking," Ashby says, sarcastically.

"Yeah, sorry. You okay?"

"Never mind, Dimples. Who's coming over?"

"A very special personage. A very, very special!"

"I got the drill, Dimples. Don't worry. When's he get here?

"Not there. Here. You gotta come back here."

"To America? That's terrific! We can spend time in L.A. and do some shopping and—"

"He's not in Los Angeles."

"New York? Wonderful! We can see a few shows—"

"Shut up and listen. He ain't in New York. Look, Ashby, this is big. What you gotta do is, just come in, do your thing, and get out fast. You understand? No shopping. No CB coming along. No nothing! Just come in, do the job and get out. Nobody can know."

"Geez, Dimples, who is it? A movie star?"

"Can't say, but there's big money it. Real—big—money."

"You know money isn't everything, Dimples," she added, with some guilt. "So how much?" Ashby added.

"A lot."

"What's a lot?"

"Don't ask."

"What does he do?"

"Everything. A lot of everything."

"And he's not in Washington?

"Not currently."

There is a long pause on the American end of the line. The faint ghost of another conversation, in French, is leaking into the line, not clear enough to understand, just a rug of sound. Ashby could hear Dimples heavy breathing.

"So, tell me, Dimples. Where exactly is he?"

"South Florida."

It took a moment for Ashby to comprehend what Dimples had said. "That guy? Holy shit!" Ashby whispered.

"Look, Just get your ass on a plane, toot-sweet."

After it was over, in back of a huge, black stretch limousine, Ashby and Dimples were enjoying the ride down the coast to the Ft. Lauderdale airport. Ashby was still slightly in shock from her historic encounter.

"I can't believe he never took his tie off, you know," she said mostly to herself.

"Forget the tie," snapped Dimples. "As far as anyone knows, it never happened, okay? Just wipe it out of your mind and get back to France."

The limousine dropped them in front of the international terminal.

"Most of your fee I wired to your account a few days ago," Dimples says as he hands her an envelope.

"I collected up front since this jerko tends to stiff anybody he works with. And here's some walk-around cash. I'm sure you'll find a good use for it. And say hi to CB for me," he says.

"So long, Dimples. I'll be in touch," Ashby says. She stands watching until the limo carrying Dimples leaves the terminal.

Ashby rushes to a cluster of credit-card pay phones, first calling American Airlines, then dialing the hotel in Nice, France.

CB picks up, and Ashby shouts, "It's me!"

"Oh, my God!" CB says. "I was just thinking about you. How'd it go?"

"How about I tell you in person? I'm at the Fort Lauderdale airport."

"Throw some stuff into a bag and meet me in New York. I'll be there way before you. I'll get us a suite at The Plaza, okay?"

"You're crazy."

"Just get here. It's my treat. I'll fill you in when I see you."

On the other end, CB screeches and attempts some half-assed excuses. She finally asks what to pack, and acts generally confused, which she generally is.

Ashby cuts her off. "Remember. The Plaza. And pack light. We can always pick up anything we need in New York."

The girls have a fantastic time, and cost be damned. They plunder Bloomingdale's and get their second wind in the best shops on upper Madison and Fifth Avenues. They see the hottest shows on Broadway, and the ticket scalpers get to know them on sight.

They are in their two-bedroom suite at The Plaza and Ashby has just hung up from her call to Dimples. She assured him things in France were fine. Had he even suspected she was in New York he would have had a heart attack.

That evening while enjoying an after-theater Martini in The Plaza's Palm Court, CB says, "You know, Ash, I've been thinking. You really should consider branching out, using your gifts for other stuff."

"Like what other stuff?"

"I don't know, like maybe—things like art restoration, cosmetic surgery. Sort of go legit! Dump the limp schlongs."

Ashby signals the waiter for another round of drinks before answering CB.

"It's not that I haven't thought about doing that," Ashby says, biting into a large olive. "I know it can work. Remember little Pinky Major?"

"Of course I do. So just imagine what you could do working with a plastic surgeon, or maybe even cancer patients."

Ashby and CB throw the ideas back and forth for another hour as they each consume another generous martini.

Getting up, they are both a bit shaky from the booze and despite the late hour, decide to stroll over to Central Park and walk for a while.

They aren't paying attention as they cross to the park.

Unfortunately, nor is the weary driver of the Taxi that hits Ashby just as she steps off the curb onto Central Park South.

And in that instant, in a storage closet in California, the burn hole in CB's chenille robe opens again. This time all by itself.

It is 3 a.m. when little Pinky Major wakes up wailing, from a nasty skinned and bleeding elbow.

In a king-sized bed in Southern Florida and behind the walls of a heavily guarded compound, a once powerful politician falls from power again—this time, to his soon-to-be-next-wife's dismay—in mid-stroke.

Later, in Rome, Italy, Don Promissori curses in Italian, then apologizes to the *prostituta*, hastily dresses and leaves the luxurious hotel suite, rushes to a nearby church to light candles in honor of the year and a half of sexual potency he had miraculously been granted.

Across the Atlantic, a Frenchman severely rebukes his son, believing the boy has defaced the fender of an expensive brown Porsche he had leaned against.

THE BIG KISS

In a penthouse high above Sunset Boulevard, Dimples rummages through his wife's dresser searching for her old, reliable appliance. He knows she will want it and hopes the batteries haven't died, along with his formerly reliable erections.

STORY IV
RETURN TO SENDER

RETURN TO SENDER

I can't help but notice the attractive, exquisitely groomed woman as she enters the hotel's crowded dining room. Thick auburn hair—slightly streaked with gray—frames a face, which I find more interesting than beautiful. The ankle-length Mink coat draped across her shoulders is already attracting a frisson of female attention.

The perfectly plumbed *maître d'hôtel* quickly materializes by her side and greets her with a warm smile. Then, with what looks to be a Bible-thick wine list clutched to his chest, he leads her through the room's maze of occupied tables.

Tucked under the woman's arm, is a long, plain cardboard mailing tube, which, given her elegant wardrobe and sophisticated demeanor, seems strangely out of place.

I soon realize their destination is an isolated area in a far corner of the room. The space is kitted out with several couches and upholstered chairs, and two large coffee tables—clearly a space intended for private use.

The woman drapes her coat across the back of one of the chairs and settles, posture perfect, onto one of the settees. She extracts a cigarette from her handbag—hesitates for a moment—then places it back. The mailing tube is propped against her knees, one end on the floor while the slender fingers of both her hands circle the tube, drumming nervously.

I sit across from my wife at a small cocktail table. The area where the woman is sitting is less than ten feet from our table. Given my position, I enjoy an unobstructed view. My wife—on the other hand—is facing me and has her back toward to scene.

We are in the hotel's dining room, after having spent a lovely, albeit, exhausting, activity-filled Sunday in Amsterdam. Once back to our hotel, tired and thirsty, we proceed directly to the dining room for a pre-dinner glass of Champagne.

The room is crowded but, as luck would have it, just as we enter, a couple vacated a small table next to one of the huge picture windows, which affords a perfect view of the Amstel River. It is the ideal spot to spend the time we had to kill, before our dinner booking.

An ex-pat 'foodie' friend has told us about Amsterdam's famous Brown Cafés—the popular sobriquet used to describe small, less-than-fancy, cozy restaurants known for outstanding food. Not unlike, he adds, the excellent Gastropubs in London.

Dinner in a 'Brown Café seems the perfect choice for our last meal in Amsterdam.

We chat about our day. Sightseeing boats and commercial barges pass leisurely on the river in front of us.

But still, my attention is continually drawn to the attractive woman sitting alone on the settee, directly in my line of sight. I feel strangely drawn to the cardboard tube and speculation as to what it might contain.

It is an unremarkable object—a standard, plain, tan-color

cardboard cylinder, roughly three feet long and three or four inches in diameter. Red plastic caps are snapped over each end, keeping whatever its contents might be in place.

Cocktail hour during the week in the large dining lounge at the rear of the Amstel Hotel, is always a scene. Starting soon after teatime, it slowly fills to overflow with cigar smoke, advertising and public relation folks, and a mixture of *road warriors*, all loud-talking, hard-drinking and business-hungry. It is red-hot commerce and ice-cold martinis.

But on Sundays—and this one is no exception—the room hosts a totally different crowd. A mixture of upper class Amsterdammers —or, as they are colloquially known, Mokummers—plus tourists like ourselves and week-end drop-ins from various parts of Europe, enjoying a short holiday, over a long weekend in a magical city.

I'm sure, as is the case with many couples, my wife and I have a little game we play when we're by ourselves in a restaurant. We randomly pick out people, then try to imagine who they might be, what kind of work they do, where they're from, that sort of thing. It can be a pleasant and entertaining way to spend time.

So, after a few minutes of watching the woman, I thought it would be fun to suggest a variation of the game. Since my wife's back is toward the woman and out of her view, I suggest the object of the game would be to guess what the contents of the tube might be.

Just then the waiter arrives to take our order. We finally settle on a very nice, and very expensive bottle of Champagne, adding as an afterthought, a plate of smoked salmon and herring.

When he leaves, I lean toward my wife to say in a low voice, "A woman came into the room a few minutes ago and I've been watching her. She's very interesting."

"Oh, great," she says. "And I thought it was me who you were quietly adoring," she adds with a smile and sips some water.

"I am always adoring you. But when you can, casually check out the woman sitting behind you. On the sofa."

"All right. But why?"

"She has this long tube."

"A long what?"

"Tube. The woman. She came in holding a tube."

"What sort of tube?" my wife asks.

"Like a long mailing tube. I thought it would be fun to try and guess what's in the tube."

"So, instead of guessing about people, we've now moved on to cardboard tubes?"

"Well, yes. It's just that the tube seems so out of place with her. (Pause). Like seeing a Nun at a boxing match.

"That is one of the dumbest analogies I've ever heard," she said.

"Yeah, okay, so maybe it is. But you get the point."

Suddenly, the waiter is back with the wine. With a slight flourish, he shows the label, I nod my approval, without understanding one scintilla of what it might have said. The cork pops, and the Champagne pours to fill the slim flutes. I taste and agree it has been an excellent choice. The plates, tableware and smoked fish are placed appropriately.

My wife and I continue.

"Okay, I'll give it a shot," she says, and turns slowly in one of those slow, casual, 'I'm-just-examining-the-ceiling-molding' kind of upper body pirouettes that allow her to glance at the woman.

Rotating back to face me, she says, "How can they let her sit alone like that? All those empty chairs, and people waiting?"

I shrug. "She's probably meeting people, you know, waiting for friends. For a party, perhaps?"

A double-decker boat packed with tourists plows upriver, quite close. Its powerful draft rattles the glass pane next to our table. A dozen random camera flashes sparkle from both its decks, each attempting to capture, for the zillionth time, the century old hotel's elegance, even though a good Post Card would have done the trick.

"Okay, take a guess. What do you think is inside?"

"Obviously, it's a present," my wife says.

"The tube is a present?"

"No, silly, the poster."

"Who said anything about a poster?" I ask. This is getting interesting.

"In the tube. A poster. Tubes like that are for posters."

"Yes, I imagine it could be a poster. But not necessarily."

"More than likely it's from one of the museums," she adds, confidently. "Probably The Van Gogh Museum. Starry Night or, how about Cornfield with Black Crows? Half the people in this room were probably at a museum today. Half the tourists in Amsterdam are probably carrying around tubes like that."

By the time I look up again, I see what I assume is the rest of her party joining the woman. They drift in rather quickly, some alone, others in little clusters of twos and threes. As they arrive, they exchange hugs and kisses. I quickly realize that I am watching a family reunion of some sort. Not discernibly different looking in Amsterdam than it would be anywhere else in the world.

Since my wife is facing me and can't see any of this, I keep her apprised of each new arrival, along with a general, running commentary on the goings on, continuing to use, of course my golf-tournament-level whisper.

"It's a family? Do they look like Mafia? Do they even have Mafia here?" my wife says.

"It just looks like a regular family. A nice affluent-looking family. Wait. This one coming in—is an older lady. Looks to be seventy-five, maybe eighty?"

"Probably the matriarch. She could be the fancy woman's mother," my wife says.

"Very possible. You can't see, but she has the same nose."

"As the woman with the tube?"

"Uh, huh. Exactly. There's teenage kid with her and he's helping the old lady with her coat. Maybe her grandson, the fancy woman's son."

"I bet it's the old lady's birthday," my wife says.

"I'd rule out a birthday. You can't see but, trust me, they don't look birthday happy."

Speculation draw us deeper into our little game, while waiters arrive to serve the family with a wide variety of fancy appetizers and trays of empty Champagne flutes. Apparently, this family gathering is not a spur of the moment get-together.

I report all this to my wife, continuing to whisper.

"What else?"

"The woman just got up. She's walking over to the old lady. She's handing her the tube. No! Wait a minute! The old lady is refusing to take the tube. She's pushing the tube away."

"She won't take it?" my wife whispered.

"Nope. She just shook her head. Patted the woman's hand, smiled and sort of turned away. *Jeezus,* now the fancy woman is crying. She's handing the tube to an older guy. From the looks of it—his age and nose—I'd say it's her older brother. And now she's leaving."

RETURN TO SENDER

"Leaving?" my wife says. "Her handbag and coat? Did she take both with her?"

"Uh-uh, just the handbag," I say.

"Then she's not leaving. Not without that coat. She's just going to the bathroom."

The woman's exit causes some visible embarrassment among the group. They all just stand, awkwardly, holding their unfilled Champagne flutes. Nor has anyone touched any of the food.

They are obviously waiting for the woman to return.

Finally, she reappears, eyes red but dry and her face composed into a weak smile.

Waiters now carefully pour the Champagne. A waiter serves some sort of juice—also in tall Champagne glasses—to the two youngest of the family, twins who look to be about seven or eight.

The woman takes back the tube from the man we assume is her brother and holding it vertically against her body with her free hand, she holds up her glass of Champagne in the gesture of a toast.

They all stand and join her. She speaks softly, in a voice I can barely hear, in a language I don't understand. The old woman remains seated and with a palsied hand, also raises her glass.

For the next hour the group chats quietly while they pick the platters clean and drink several more bottles of Champagne.

While this is going on we fabricate various silly scenarios around what is happening, and the possible contents of the tube. First my wife—still insisting it was the older woman's birthday—made a fanciful case for the tube containing an expensive fly-rod which the old lady can't accept because of a painful arthritic condition, which prevents her from pursuing what had been her lifelong passion for fly fishing.

I, on the other hand, speculate it might contain several cans of tennis balls since they could approximate the tube's length and breadth. Either that or one of those long, thin spy-glasses. Possibly an umbrella.

As we work through our bottle of Champagne and plates of smoked fish, our guesses about the contents of the tube become even more outrageous.

Eventually the woman with the tube, must have signaled for the check, because a waiter appears and hands her a long slip of paper. She gives it a cursory glance, hands it back, along with a stack of Gilders, counted out from her handbag. A quick pursing of her lips and a dismissive hand movement silently instructs the waiter to keep the change.

The waiter bows, acknowledging what must have been a generous gratuity. That, in turn, seems to signal for the group to ready themselves to leave.

"They're finished," I whisper.

For the next few minutes, I watch as they struggle into outer coats, scarves, hats and gloves. The old lady is carefully helped by the young man we assume is her grandson.

The woman, enclosed once again inside her fur, stubs out the cigarette she is smoking, picks up the mailing tube and, with the rest trailing behind, leaves the lounge headed in the direction of the hotel's front entrance.

The vacated space is quickly and efficiently bussed and set-up for whatever group will be next to arrive.

I sit silently for a few minutes, sipping the last of my Champagne and contemplating what I have just witnessed.

After a few minutes it suddenly dawns on me.

"By golly, I know what's in the tube," I declare, whispering no longer necessary.

"Trust me, it's a poster," my wife says, with a smug certainty.

"No, I'm positive it's not a poster and I know what it is."

"Well, I guess we'll never know," she said, taking a sip from her Champagne.

I take out my pen and write something on one of the paper cocktail napkins, then fold it.

"What are you writing?" my wife asks.

"Try to guess what I'm thinking is in the tube?"

"You've got to be kidding?"

"No. I wrote my guess on the napkin, so you'll know I didn't cheat or anything."

"What's the difference? We'll never find out and I still think it was a poster."

"I know. But wouldn't it still be fun just to guess?" I say.

"Actually, I would prefer another glass of Champagne instead."

As I mentioned before, the large window next to our table looked out on the Amstel River. Between the river and the window—behind which we are sitting—is a dock about ten or fifteen feet wide that runs the length of the building. It is quickly turning dark, and a line of lights recessed into the wooden planking along the dock automatically come on. Other lights on the buildings across the river light up, as well, along with countless others that sketch the outline of a nearby bridge. We have a ring-side view of a glorious sight.

Just then, some movement at the far end of the dock catches my eye. I see it's a group of people walking toward us, single file, down a short flight of stairs that offer access to the dock from the river side of the hotel.

It's the woman, and she is leading the group, mailing tube clutched to her chest.

They march slowly in our direction along the lighted dock to a point almost directly in line with and just below where we are sitting. They stop and face the river. It is totally dark now and the wind is coming up. The Barges, passing in both directions, are looking quite festive now, outlined as they are with strings of light. Their wake causes the dock to move slightly, up and down.

I see that my wife and I are not the only patrons who notice the group standing on the dock. Even the waiters stop to look.

The group forms a half-circle around the woman, all facing the river, their backs toward us. The woman grasps the cardboard tube with one hand and with the other, twists off one red-capped end. Then, with only a moment of hesitation, she swings the tube in an overhand, casting motion, aiming toward the river. She holds fast to the tube and its contents shoot out with some force—a large, grainy teardrop—and for a split second, it hangs, suspended in the air, neither moving forward, nor falling.

Suddenly a blast of wind, possibly the strong draft from a passing barge slaps the grainy mass and spreads it out like a blooming flower, pushing it back toward the dock.

A dozen bodies freeze in shock as a blanket of ashes is suddenly blown back onto them. In the lounge there is an audible and simultaneous intake of breath.

No one moves. No one speaks. Even the barges seem not to move.

And then, although the thick glass blocks any sound, we see the old lady began a pumping up and down movement of her shoulders. At first, it appears she might be crying. Then it is clear she is laughing. A full laugh. And crying a little, too. And the rest of the family, they are also laughing and crying a little, too. Brushing the ashes from their clothing, holding, and hugging each other. Releasing the incredible tension that has been stored up for God knows how long.

Of course, their reaction is contagious and those of us inside come out of our momentary shock and laugh right along, and some cry a little, as well. A few of us clap and wave. The people on the dock become aware that we are watching, and they wave back. The woman is smiling and laughing and crying.

That's when I unfold the napkin and hold it so my wife can see my prophetic message and with eyes wet with tears, she leans over and kisses me.

STORY V
JOHN DENVER
AND THE OVENS OF WESTPORT

JOHN DENVER AND THE OVENS OF WESTPORT

The Year: 1975

By the way," my wife mumbled through a yellow pencil clamped between her teeth. "When he comes upstairs, whatever you do, don't talk to him. Don't start. Not a word. Not even a hello."

My wife was at the kitchen table, starting and stopping a cassette tape player. Going forward and back. Playing and re-playing snippets from a John Denver song. Converting his recording into simple chords for her young guitar students.

I was standing on a low stool, a few feet away, wielding a razor blade, attempting to remove four slivers of Scotch tape that once held our kindergartner's finger painting onto the front of the wall cabinet. The child was now in middle school and the tape had, long ago, fossilized.

"It won't come off! Trust me, you're going to fuck up the finish," my wife declared in her special way that demanded our seconds meet to arrange a duel.

"It's—coming—off," I whispered through clenched teeth, more to myself than to anyone else. "The little—mothers are—coming—off!"

"...*COLD HERE IN THE CI-TY...*" John Denver's voice sang out from the recorder.

Suddenly the oil furnace in the basement rumbled to life with a deep, vibrating shudder that felt a lot like little aftershocks we'd learned to live with when we made our home in Los Angeles.

"Thank God it's fixed," my wife said, revealing a deep superstition that all good comes from Him. "We'll probably have a heat wave tomorrow," she added, noting an equally deep superstition that God probably thinks too much good, isn't too good.

"*ALWAYS SEEMS ...*" John sings. She hits some buttons that force John to repeat. "*...ALWAYS SEEMS ...*"

"Why shouldn't I talk to him? The furnace man?" I ask, my face screwed into a sour expression.

"Because," she says, as if the answer is obvious, "He's filthy and a German. Probably a Nazi and, if you get him started, he won't stop talking, with his horrible accent, and he has this crazy scar on his head. Just don't start is all."

I stood up there, the razor poised in mid air, trying to decide whether to deliver a lecture about equality and stereotypical narrow mindedness. I was tempted since there's a psychological advantage to speaking from a higher position than one's audience.

However, at that moment the furnace man appeared in the doorway.

She was right in one respect: He was filthy! Dirt, grease, grime, grit—he was the ultimate "before" of a TV detergent commercial. And it didn't stop with his clothing. It continued onto his neck and face and ears and hair, his wrists and hands and shoes. He brought to mind a used pipe cleaner.

"I fix it, mister," he said in a thick accent and a downward chop of his head. "When oil burns it's leaving a—a," He grabbed for the English like a child goes after a goldfish.

"Sludge?" I prompt.

"A sludge! Yes, a sludge on the bottom. And it builds up thick but then it don't burn good, you see? Not burn enough for nothing!"

His large, hooded eyes drifted over toward the coffee pot. He had the kind of skin; the kind of face, that always looks very close. Large pores. Thick hair stubble.

"Could I—you mind, I would please like a cup coffee?"

His question made me realize I'd been staring at him.

"Oh yeah, sure," I said. My head nodded once. I got off the stool and poured him a cup.

I heard my wife expel her 'oh, shit' moan.

' ... *IT ALWAYS SEEMS THAT WAY...*' John sang out of her little machine.

"The papers," The man said, pointing behind him, into the dining room.

My face showed I didn't understand.

"I put papers to walk on. I don't make any mess. I walk on papers.

"Oh, sure. No problem," I laughed.

'...*BEEN THINKING A-BOUT... YOU ... EVERYDAY...*' John continued.

The fingers that took the coffee cup from me were thick and square and the nails black and split. One finger was missing to the first joint and the scarred skin on the stump had long ago been pulled closed, like the top on a laundry bag.

"Where are you from?" I asked, sipping my own coffee.

"DAMN!" My wife said, loudly and we both turned toward her. "The machine," she lied, with a half smile

I made a face at her that screamed, "Wrong again and I'll prove it—just like the damned scotch tape on the cabinet you swore, would never come off."

"I come from Poland. The town, is gone now. The Nazis make it go away." The furnace man made a motion with his hand like a child slowly erasing a work off a blackboard.

'... *EVERYDAY...'* John sang low and slow.

The dirty furnace man carefully placed his empty cup on the counter next to him. He hadn't moved from his spot since he came off the paper trail and into the kitchen. It was as if he thought the dirt might drip off onto the floor like water.

"You come down in basement, see how good I fix," he said, quite expansively. He was proud and I didn't have the heart to ignore his work.

My wife shook her head and curled one side of her mouth into a mocking smile. I somehow pitied her for that.

I followed the man along the paper path, already ripped here and there, where his heavy shoes had pressed the cheap newsprint into the thick nap of the carpet.

"It will be good now. Fixed good," he said addressing the furnace complex, when we arrived.

It was true. The oil furnace was burning with a strong, steady roar. In fact, the whole room was transformed. I had been down there the week before looking for an extension cord and the furnace room had been a musty, filthy mess. Now it was spotless. I admired it in a physical way, with nods and noises of appreciation so that he might see and know. We both stood there after that in self-conscious silence.

"Well, uh—what happened after Hitler—you know, after he came?" I asked, not being able to deal with the silence.

He grunted a small laugh, more of memory than comedy.

"I escaped," he said, raising his shoulders toward his ears and holding his hands out, palms up.

"Where to?"

"...to Jerusalem. It was 1939 then."

"You're a Jew?" I asked, the pitch of my voice up slightly with surprise.

"Yes," he said, with a shrug and a smile. "The British, they were at Jerusalem then. They take me into British army. I work hard and they make me a sergeant. I went with army six years. We fight all the way to Italy."

As he spoke he fingered, no, he caressed the scar on his forehead. The one my wife had called crazy.

"I was lucky one," he continued, "many men get killed. Too many killed. The English put me in front often. It was their little joke, you know: The Jew sergeant. I am lucky that Germans do things too much, you know. Too good, sometimes. They shelled and bomb us deep. Way past front lines where I was. The British officers who are far back, the ones who laughed, they got killed pretty quick."

"And afterwards, did you go back to Israel?" I asked. I was leaning up against the recently cleaned door frame. The single light bulb over the furnace cast weak light over the man and seemed to darken the dirt on his face.

"No," he said, slowly shaking his head, "first I go back to Poland. To town where I am born."

He was quiet for some time and I could see he'd fallen deeply into a memory. I said nothing.

He reached down and absently pulled open the small, cast iron door on the furnace. The steel pear-shape spring handle clanked. A clean, blue flame threw tie-dyed light over his body. The flames grew more audible.

Finally he spoke."The SS, they built a camp—a crematory, like Auschwitz, where my town was. The flesh smell was still thick. Some half dead survivors still were living there, waiting for God knows what. The big ovens were still hot. They had burned so long, like hell burns, you know. The bricks would never be cool again.

"The SS kept records of everything—everything. I search the records day and night for seven days. So many names, mister. From all over Europe. On the Sabbath I found them."

The low roar of the flames in the small oil furnace mixed with his breathing. A muffled echo of John Denver singing upstairs. No discernible words, just muffled tone.

"The names were all, you know, together, the way they arrested them, I think."

"My mama, my papa," he moved his head up and down ticking them off. "My six brothers, my little twin sisters. Others, too. Relatives. Our Rabbi. Friends. Sarah, the first girl I kissed. My teachers. All into the flames."

I stood very still. Heat from the furnace filled the small room. The ice in my stomach melted into tears and blurred my vision.

He took a deep, long breath and cleared his head with a small, abrupt movement. "I went crazy then. Some of the SS men were still there with the Americans. Prisoners, waiting for trial. I try hard to kill them. The police, they stop me and I get this," he traced, the scar with his hand.

Neither of us spoke for a moment and then I noticed his hand, still on the door, so close to the flame that the small hairs on the back of his fingers and hand were beginning to singe and smoke, slightly. The smell was nauseating and hit me like a slap.

"Your hand!" I yelled, pointing. He looked down and absently brushed the back slowly, with his other dirty, callused hand.

"It is nothing. It happens, it is nothing," he said.

"When I am recovering from my head, I made my way back

to Israel. They were a new State and the British were gone. So now Israel has army and they need men like me, you know. They tell me that if I stay I must go back into army. But I have enough army so I come to America.

"It was lonely," he said nodding his head and pouting out his thick lower lip. "But, you know, mister, I wanted to be alone. I had no trade so I get job working with this," he pointed to the flame in the furnace. "With flames and ovens. It made me feel close to them."

"No one bothers me here. I work near the warm of the flame and it—makes them all seem, so close. Not so dead.

"It is silly, you know. Maybe a bit—" he touched his head near his ear," meshuganah." He rolled the Yiddish word meaning crazy across his lips in a whisper and smiled.

Light reflected of his face and the oily dirt on his skin and clothes glistened and shone. The wet tracks of tears rolled over the dirt from his eyes to his chin.

"Meshuganah! That's what most people think I am. I come and put down my papers and go into cellars and I spend my days with the flames.

"I talk to my brothers and sisters and argue Torah with my papa. I talk about recipes with my mama. I sing with my little sisters and the days go quick. I make it nice for them."

For the second time I looked around the furnace room. It was very clean. The beams and furnace had been vacuumed; boxes were piled together. Scrap lumber was lined up neatly in the corner. Useless debris had been removed.

Then it hit me. The papers he laid, they were for the homeowner. A nice thoughtful touch. The spotless furnace and furnace room, the strong, steady flame, that was for them. For his mother and his father. For all of the ones he love who had been murdered.

I moved my hands indicating the room, "Everything…all this—it's like—it's for—them, isn't it."

He looked at me with a small smile, walked past me and waited just outside the door of the furnace room. I, too, turned and left. As I passed him he snapped the light switch and shut the door, softly.

Upstairs, at the back door, he paused. "Thank you mister, for the coffee. I will see you, God willing, next winter for cleaning. The furnace is fixed and good."

He walked away several steps and turned back toward me. I could feel the thought forming in his mind under the grime.

"Don't worry," I said before he could ask, before he even had to ask, "I promise, I'll keep the furnace room clean for you." He smiled and waved.

I was still standing at the door as his old, dirty truck belched out of our driveway. '... *BUT MORE THAN ANY-Y-THING ELSE ... I'M SOR-RY FOR MY SELF ... 'CAUSE YOU'RE NOT HERE ... WITH ME ...'* I heard John Denver lament from inside the kitchen.

JOHN DENVER AND THE OVENS OF WESTPORT

Words to song, I'M SORRY, Copyright 1975, Cherry Lane Music.

STORY VI
A PICK-UP AT ROSETTA'S

A PICK-UP AT ROSETTA'S

Forster spun through the revolving doors just as a late winter snow started falling—heavy and wet. He settled onto a stool at the far end of the long, polished mahogany bar and ordered a drink.

The barman, name of Pomeroy, took his order with a nod, splashed a generous amount of Vodka into a shaker, added ice and a 'mist' of Vermouth from a tiny atomizer, clamped the works between two beefy mitts, and pumped it hard, to a tune only he could hear.

Forster waiting, gazing absently at the gray blur of Friday's after-work crowd rushing past Rosetta's front window—fogged to translucency with condensation.

Shortly, Pomeroy, in an impressive display of expert mixology, slowly poured the ice-cold mixture into the frosted glass, allowing the last drop to push the liquid's level slightly above its rim, just short of spilling, thanks to some obscure law of physics. Forster had to bend to the glass for his first sip, not daring to try it any other way. Pomeroy then slid a small napkin with three skewered olives next to the drink.

When not traveling on business, Forster showed up at Rosetta's on a fairly regular basis. It was close to his apartment, Pomeroy made a decent martini, and the food was always dependable. Even so, the barman never seemed to recognize Forster from one visit to the next, which suited Forster just fine.

In truth, it wasn't Pomeroy's fault—Forster was just not a particularly memorable man. Not that anything was wrong with the way he looked. Not at all.

It was just that he appeared to be so—unremarkable. Medium height; medium build; eyes that might have been brown or hazel, or gray. His hair wasn't thick, nor was it thin. It was just, you know, plain, mid-brownish hair. His clothing was of good quality, but with an off-the-rack look. Even his expensive shoes were often a bit scuffed.

Forster's persona was unremarkable, as well. He wasn't funny, or loud, or boorish, nor was he quiet or shy, either. He could keep up his end of any conversation, mostly by carefully listening, which seemed to surprise and delight most people. One could spend an hour, or a day with Forster and, the following week, not recognize him at a cocktail party.

Fortunately, given Forster's line of work, this rendered him somewhere close to perfection. It was as if nature had designed Forster to be that way: like one of those little undersea creatures that, when faced with a predator, can suddenly look like a shell or a rock, or puff-up to a more intimidating size. It was a vital function for survival.

Forster checked his watch. It was a bit early and he couldn't decide if he was hungry, bored, or just tired.

It had been a quick, two-day trip—much more difficult than he had anticipated, ending with a tedious drive back to the city that, thanks to a collision on the turnpike, trapped Forster behind the wheel of his rental car for what seemed like, forever.

He sipped at his drink and contemplated the possible places where he might go—to get away, unwind and soak-in the sun for a few weeks. He needed a break. Desperately. His choices were, of course, endless—there was plenty of money—yet, at the same time, nothing that came to mind seemed very appealing.

His thoughts were interrupted by Pomeroy, asking if he cared for a refill, which he did. Then, looking around, Forster realized that during his musings, most of the stools along the mahogany bar were now occupied.

Just then a large man stopped next to Forster—by one of the few stools not taken. He shook snow from his coat, which smelled of wet wool. The outside cold radiated from him like an aura. As he prepared to be seated, a harsh, muffled ringtone sounded and the man frantically juggled through the pockets of his overcoat, in order to answer the call.

"Yeah! (pause) I AM here, dammit! At the bar. (pause) Well how the fuck should I know you already had a table? (pause) I'll be right there. (pause) Yes. A Bourbon. Make it a double."

As the man left, without a word, a woman materialized in his place. From what little he could see, not unattractive. Thick glasses. Maybe mid-forties. A heavy layer of snow covered a knitted hat pulled low over her head. She was encased in a black, ankle-length, down-filled 'bubble' coat. A heavy scarf made several loops around her neck. She held a briefcase in a mittened hand.

"Excuse me," she said, addressing Forster. "Do you know if that man's coming back?"

"Doubtful," Forster said. "I believe it's all yours."

She proceeded to unwrap. A full head of blond hair spilled out from under the hat, then a full figure in a simple, long sleeve, black jersey dress emerged from under the bulky coat. She reminded Forster of a butterfly emerging from its chrysalis. She draped the bulky coat over the stool, wet side down, and wiggled onto the barstool.

Forster observed her reflection in the mirrored bar. She was, in fact, very attractive.

Pomeroy appeared in a flash, and took her order.

Once her Martini arrived, and she'd taken a few sips, she and Forster slid into a casual conversation—the kind of chitchat strangers, perched on adjoining bar stools, tend to have: do you live in the city—Forster, yes, the woman, no. How crappy the weather had been lately. Broadway shows. Recent movies. That sort of thing.

Her given name was Logan. It was Scottish, and her mother's maiden name. Not married—she claimed—sold computer software. In the city on business. Lives in one of the square, Mid-Western states.

Forster, as usual, did most of the listening.

Time passed quickly, during which, the bar gradually cleared of its suburban commuters and pre-theater goers.

"God," Logan suddenly exclaimed. "I haven't stopped talking. You haven't told me a thing about yourself—and, of course, I didn't give you much of a chance. Someone told me once that getting a word in, when I'm talking, is like trying to merge onto the Hollywood freeway from an on ramp."

Forster laughed, having experienced the analogy, first hand. Logan took a deep breath. "Okay, now it's your turn. What do you do?"

Forster looked at her carefully for some seconds, not saying anything, just thinking—slowly weighing the wisdom, the pros and cons of what he was—for God-only-knows-what-reason—tempted to tell her. Maybe it was his mood, his recent feelings of frustration, of exhaustion. Was it something about this woman, he wondered, that made him even consider it? He knew he was crawling out onto a very thin limb. One that could conceivably break, and then where would he be? Oh, fuck it, he thought.

He leaned toward her, reducing the space between them to something much more intimate—he caught the subtle scent of her perfume as he said, in a whisper, "I'm an assassin."

There was a short beat of silence—enough for Logan's eyebrows to rise, making her eyes saucer-like. She leaned back slightly, observing Forster as if he were a newspaper page she was attempting to get into focus. And then a roar of laughter rose from deep inside and burst out from between her full red lips and brilliantly white teeth.

"That's one of the funniest, craziest things a guy's ever said to me—in a bar, anyway. I must admit it's very creative. But seriously, what do you really do?"

Forster took a bite from an olive and chewed it slowly, never taking his eyes off Logan. "Your reaction is interesting. What I just told you is something I've told very few people. Maybe two, or three come to mind. But every one had the same reaction: just like you, they laughed. They didn't for a single second even consider I was being serious. I must be joking, right?"

"Of course—you're joking," Logan said. "If you were an assassin, why would you tell anyone? You'd be crazy. Someone asks you what you do and you say you're an assassin—it's got to be for the effect it has, right? It's a 'pick-up' line extraordinaire. A conversational ice-breaker," Logan said.

"I agree with you. Everything you just said is reasonable and logical. Nevertheless, what I told you is true. I really am. That's the simple fact."

"You're really, really serious?"

"Really, really. Yes."

"Okay, let's pretend you are what you say. Why on earth would you tell me? Why would you tell anybody? Killing people is against the law."

"Lots of things are against the law, you know. But people do them anyway. As for murder—look what atrocities politicians commit and get away with."

"True. But you don't know me. I'm a stranger. I could be an undercover cop! Or—I don't know— I could just call the police. Turn you in. You could go to jail. Like forever."

Forster smiled. "You think so? Okay, let's pretend a cop just walked in. You wave him over and tell him what? Exactly what will you tell him? 'Officer, this man just told me he's an assassin.' The cop's going to think that you're drunk or some sort of nut case or, more than likely, that I'm trying to pick you up using a very dumb, albeit, as you point out, a very creative line. The last thing he's going to do is cuff me and haul me into jail."

"But you've got to admit, if you did actually kill someone, then you would go to jail, right?"

"But only if I got caught."

Logan thought about that for a moment, still not completely taken in by Forster's claim.

"For argument's sake, pretend I believe you. So, give me a for-instance—who did you—or do you assassinate?"

Forster shrugged. "It varies. There are individuals, corporations, governments—you'd be surprised at the number of people—entities—all over the world who, at some point in time, and for any number of reasons, need a—shall we say, need an problem resolved."

"And they call you?"

"No, no, no. They contact someone, who contacts someone else, who talks to other people—who, in turn, contact me. I never know who originates the contract. I simply remove the problem."

"You just wipe someone off the face of the earth, as if they were a word chalked on a blackboard?"

"That's a graphic way of putting it, but yes."

"And the morality of that? Isn't it a problem?"

"I've never been a religious man. Let's just say, it's never presented a problem for me. I'm certainly not losing any sleep over it."

"And you get paid for this."

"Oh, yes. I'm paid a great deal. More than you can imagine."

Logan was silent for a long time. Finally, "How did you—you know, get in to this? I mean, it's not like something you can major in, in college."

Forster took a final sip of his drink, sat up straight and twisted a bit, working the kinks out of his back.

"Oh, God, Logan, it's a long story and very honestly, its been a tedious day, and I'm really hungry."

"We could go someplace and have a bit. It's not like I have anyplace special to be," Logan said.

Forster hadn't been with a woman for a long time. Besides, Logan was attractive and he was feeling very comfortable with her.

"Tell you what. If you're game, my apartment is a few blocks away and I can get some Chinese delivered, that is, as long as you're not afraid to be alone with an assassin."

The next morning Logan awoke early, showered and dressed while Forster was still sleeping. She cleared away the detritus of the prior evening, dumping the empty Chinese food containers, and a half-dozen empty Dos Equis bottles. She found the bread and put on coffee. Forster padded into the kitchen, giving her what would easily qualify as a 'shit-eaten grin—a long kiss, then left to shower.

Ten minutes later they sat at the small dining table, Forster in a bathrobe, freshly scrubbed, and Logan, in the black jersey dress, looking as lovely as she had the night before.

She'd noted the time. There was a flight to catch in a few hours and she still had to gather her things from her hotel. Forster understood, but was still sad to think of her leaving. His lovely, albeit brief, encounter with Logan had made him realize how lonely he was—and how he had come to accept that state of being as normal.

Logan buttered a piece of toast and silently sipped coffee. She poured orange juice into two glasses and pushed one toward Forster who, after swallowing a mouthful of toast, drank it down, reaching out with his free hand to touch her arm.

Logan promised to call when she landed, and planned to be back in a few weeks. Forster wrote down all of Logan's contact information as she recited it.

Forster was about to say how much he would miss her when suddenly he grunted from a sharp pain that shot through his gut. Sweat beaded across his face and ran down his chin. His breathing became labored.

Not a God damned heart attack! Please, not now, for God's sake!

Forster took deep breaths and the pain began to lessen. But something wasn't right. He looked up at Logan. She was standing now, across the table from Forster. Her face showing no trace of alarm.

And then, a horrible realization. "Oh, Christ, Logan—not the—juice?"

"Sorry, Forster. It's not personal—you know that. Really."

"I—I don'—understand?" Forster struggled with the words. "What about—didn't you—what—about last night?"

Logan chuckled, a reaction that hurt Forster more than the pain. "I was bored. You can relate to that, can't you? We're in a lonely business. Like the song says, even cowgirls get the blues."

"But why?"

Logan shrugged. "I guess you were somebody's problem. And face it, Forster, you're not the only assassin."

"Who?"

"No idea. Hell, you know the drill. I got a call, we settled on a price—and, if it's any satisfaction, you were worth a bundle. That was that. But I promise, it will be fast. Professional courtesy, and all. Some new synthetic stuff I've been using. Very little pain. Works on your motor control. You'll pass out soon. I'm told it's easier if you don't fight it." Logan turned and walked into the living room.

Forster sat, motionless in his chair. He was beginning to feel like a statue. The initial stab of pain was fading, but now his limbs were becoming heavy. With a great deal of effort he slowly reached under the table to a small shelf and, with incredible difficulty, willed his fingers to curl around the grip of the tiny Beretta 22a, which he kept stashed there for an emergency—and this certainly qualified. The silencer attached to it was longer than the pistol. He laboriously jerked his arm out, up, and over the rim of the table, where it lay, as heavy and stiff as a bar of steel. Forster pushed his feet back, slowly, under his chair, sweat dripped down his face, then tilted forward, just enough to slide off his chair, to his knees, causing his stiff arm, still on the table, to lever upward.

Logan, dressed to leave, came back into the room and watched him, fascinated, a smile on her lips.

"Come on, Forster, you're in no condition to shoot anyone.

Even if you could aim it and pull the trigger, which you can't—a Beretta 22a is like a peashooter."

Forster's rigid arm and gun hand were now tilted up at an angle toward Logan, and he willed his finger to apply pressure on the trigger—willed it with all his might. The suppressed report was so non-lethal sounding, as to be almost comical—the spitting of an alpaca. Whatever his shot hit in the other room made a shattering sound.

The diminutive caliber of the tiny pistol required extreme accuracy for any hope of a kill shot, something Forster was no longer capable of. He was barely able to keep the pistol in Logan's direction, let alone actually aim the damned thing.

With a final burst of effort he managed to jerk his arm to the left, trying as best he could to compensate for the first miss.

Logan took a quick step toward Forster. "Okay, cowboy, enough's, enough. Don't fight it. Just relax."

Another spitting sound, accompanied the last shot before his finger lost all ability, or hope of ever moving again.

His vision was blurring rapidly, and the details of Logan fused into a vague, gray outline. But then, a crescent of brightness suddenly arched in a long crescent, away from the blur.

By some miracle of chance, Forster's bullet, barely skimming beneath Logan's ear, had apparently nicked her neck, and severed her carotid artery. She slid, slowly, down the wall to a sitting position on the floor across from Forster, a look of utter astonishment, mixed with what looked like admiration spread across her face.

"Fuck," she said.

And they watched each other die.

STORY VII
UNCLE WALT

UNCLE WALT

I clearly recall a time when my birthdays were in single digits. America was still crawling out from under the depression while being sucked into another World War. Life was a struggle, at best. So, it wasn't unusual for a family to have a relative or two living with them.

That was around the time my Uncle Walt moved in with us. He was my mom's younger brother and was with us to spend time with his sister—aka, my mom—waiting to turn eighteen so he could get into the Army.

We celebrated his birthday at the end of November, and it seemed that as soon as the candles were blown out and the cake eaten, he took off like a shot to enlist. His Army physical was on December 11, 1941, the day America declared war on Germany, four days after the Japs attacked Pearl Harbor.

Uncle Walt was with us for six months. But to me, it was like a lifetime. I grew to love my uncle. He treated me like a buddy, not a baby. No cheek pinching or phony baloney. On weekends we'd go to the movies and after, sit at the counter of our local Five & Dime and have milk shakes, eat peanut butter crackers, and talk about the movie and news reels we'd just seen. He knew a lot about movie stuff and told me he wanted to go into that business when he got out of the Army. I learned a lot from him and never looked at movies the same way, again.

Uncle Walt also introduced me to all kinds of strange foods. It turned out that lots of stuff I thought I'd hate, were really pretty good. And he very subtlety instilled in me an appreciation for classical music just by pointing out how the stories I listened to on radio relied on classical music to make the shows more dramatic.

I cried the day he left for induction and boot camp. The last time I saw Walt—at least what I think of as "The Old Walt"—was when he'd finished boot camp and specialty training and had a few weeks furlough before shipping out for England. He looked so great in his leather Air Force jacket, polished boots, and fresh, new Corporal's stripes.

Uncle Walt wrote a lot of letters to mom and pops from overseas. He always included a note just for me, which I read over and over and collected in a cigar box where I kept my treasures. But like all young kids, I easily found where pops and mom hid Walt's letters and read every word. Uncle Walt's handwriting was the worst!

According to Walt's reporting, he was taking a lot of heat in boot camp, what with being from New York, small—he was only 5'8" at 150 pounds, and a Jew, to boot. I knew first-hand the thing about people hating Jews since we did live across the street from a Catholic school and I would get pushed around quite a bit, just for supposedly killing Christ, which anyone could tell you, I had nothing to do with.

On the other hand, the being from New York thing was, at the time, a total mystery to me. But, as my mom assured me, my Uncle Walt was a "tough cookie."

Pops said, "Walt may be small but he's as strong as a Belgian draft horse and just crazy enough to grab every opportunity to prove he's the toughest, bravest guy in his squadron, even if he has to do it with his fists."

After boot camp all recruits had to take an aptitude test and based on the results, classifications were made for what the next level of their training would be. Rarely did the tests mean much. The men coming out of basic training were just moved around like chess pieces—sent to wherever the military wanted them. At the time, The Army Air Force needed bodies to man the growing number of B-17s rolling off the assembly lines, and Uncle Walt wanted to fly.

Now, the assignment thought to be the worst one could get on a B-17 crew, was the Ball Turret Gunner.

The ball turret was a cramped glass and metal ball that hung from the bottom of the B-17. Almost anyone of sound mind didn't want anything to do with the job. It was rarely discussed, but the life expectancy of a ball turret gunner in a combat situation was said to be 37 seconds. It may have been apocryphal to some extent, but even so. Better men than Walter had gone to extreme lengths to avoid ball turret gunner training. Shooting themselves in the leg or arm, even going A.W.O.L.—and facing a Courts martial—none of these acts of desperation seemed out of the question. If there was any way to avoid being a ball turret gunner, it was considered worth it.

To the powers that be, Uncle Walt was a perfect patsy for the job. He was short, skinny and seemingly fearless.

But even before he was told about the assignment for the dreaded ball turret training, Uncle Walt went to the squadron commander and volunteered.

So, Uncle Walt, his transit documents in hand, traveled by Greyhound bus to Las Vegas where men like Walt were trained to be ball turret gunners. Soon after finishing his training, Uncle Walt got his Gunner wings, his corporal stripes and, along with a few thousand other GIs, sailed to England where he joined his B-17 crew. It wasn't too long before they started flying missions over Germany, with Uncle Walt, curled in a tight fetal position inside his glass and metal ball, suspended from the bottom of a 65,000-pound Super Fortress.

On his tenth mission, Uncle Walt's plane was shot down. He was fortunate enough to barely get himself out of the ball terret in time to survive the crash landing. But both his legs were badly broken. Seven of the ten-man crew were killed and the remaining three—Uncle Walt, the tail gunner, and the navigator, were quickly captured, and spent two years in a German P.O.W. camp where Uncle Walt got a minimum of medical care and an inhuman amount of physical abuse.

After the camp was liberated, Uncle Walt spent more than a year in a military hospital outside of London where his body was healed as much as it ever would be.

His mind was another story.

Once back in the States and discharged from service, Uncle Walt came to live with us again. Pops made a place for him up in our small attic. It wasn't fancy but mom made sure it was comfortable. There was a soft, over-stuffed lounge chair, a Philco radio and a single bed with a good mattress, a coffee table with lots of magazines and a bunch of the comic books Walt enjoyed reading. It was a cozy, warm and dry space. Even had a rug and a small table with a large ash tray for Uncle Walt to use when he cleaned out his pipe, which he smoked, non-stop, from morning until he went to bed at night.

But Uncle Walt was not the same. Not even close. He would spend most of his days in his lounger, listening to the radio, smoking his pipe, and thumbing through his magazines and comic books until the pages were as soft as worn dollar bills. He also talked to himself. It wasn't exactly talk I could initially make out, more like animated mumbling that I eventually came to understand. Sort of. Some nights we could hear him mumbling and crying in his sleep.

Back in those days there were no "Assisted Living" places to take care of the millions of "Walts" that were back from the war. Pops had heard about a few fancy places—Sanitariums—that were for those who could pay the price for deluxe care.

All Uncle Walt had was his attic room. No tennis courts or ceramics classes or nurses to push him around in a wheelchair or shrinks and social worker to help heal his mind.

Any effective drugs which might have allowed my Uncle Walt, or any of the other "Walts" to lead a half-way normal life had yet to be developed.

Millions of families across America were living with similar situations, and, thankfully, most of their "Walts" healed and were able to move forward with their lives.

Throngs of veterans swarmed back to colleges and trade schools, thanks to the G.I. Bill. But many—too many—were like my Uncle Walt, rocking and smoking away each day and mumbling to themselves for the rest of their lives.

So, the various "Uncle Walts" as I called them, sat alone. Some were fortunate and had some friends and family—maybe school mates, elderly moms and dads, or grandkids—who would come and sit with them for a while and listen to their first-person reports of the sad glory and ironic farce of war. Or maybe just keep them company and let their Walt win a game of checkers.

UNCLE WALT

Back then, my best friend was called Wings—his real name was Sam, but we all had nicknames. Anyway, his was Wings because he loved to make model airplanes. Not like the plastic model kits of today—with crappy stamped-out parts that any idiot could snap together. These planes were made from balsa wood, and each part had to be carefully cut out with a razor blade and glued together. Anyway, me and Wings were close, and most days we'd try to spend some time in the attic shooting the breeze with my Uncle Walt.

Uncle Walt was maybe twenty-five at the time? But he looked ancient, like someone three times twenty-five. What little walking he did was with the help of two canes. What hair he had left was wispy white and his speech—if one wasn't accustomed to hearing it—was difficult to understand.

But we liked being with him. Also, it didn't hurt that he let Wings and me smoke with him. We would sit, fascinated, and watch him roll our cigarettes. If he was in the mood, he'd do it with one hand. He used special little papers and pinches of Sir Walter Raleigh pipe tobacco. Wings and me, we'd light up, using a wooden match we'd fish out of the big box of Diamond Kitchen Matches he kept next to him, and puff away, trying not to cough too much.

Uncle Walt liked listening to what he called, "his stories" on the radio. Depending on what time we were with him, maybe we'd hear *The Lone Ranger*, *The Fat Man* or *Doctor Danger*. And, if we hit the one time of the week when it was broadcast, we'd turn out Uncle Walt's lamp, lay on the rug and listen to *The Shadow*. As soon as it went on, we'd all deepen our voices and, in a serious tone, whisper, "*Who knows what evil lurks in the hearts of man? The Shadow knows!*" Then we'd laugh like madmen and cough on our own cigarette smoke. Uncle Walt would laugh, too. At least try to in his own way.

Sometimes when we went to see Uncle Walt—lots of times,

actually—he would give us money to buy his favorite tobacco. And, in his strange voice way, he'd say, "Go down to Grossman's"—Grossman was the neighborhood pharmacist—"and you ask him, *'You got Sir Walter Raleigh in a can?'* And if he says yeah, you tell him, *'Let him out, cause he's suffocatin' in there.'*"

We would always all chime in to say the last line along with Uncle Walt. And then we'd roll around the floor and laugh so hard, we'd practically puke.

I was about eight or nine when my Pops enlisted in the army. Technically, he was exempt and didn't have to go. At thirty-five, he was over the age limit, married and with a kid. But pops was a talker and men were needed. So, when he volunteered and was initially turned down, he just talked and talked until they took him.

I was always proud of pops for that.

Me and mom were left to keep the home fires burning—an expression that sometimes gave me nightmares. I would wake up in a sweat from one of my nightmares and try to think about what I would do if one of those "home fires" I was meant to keep burning, would actually burn? Especially, if the only way out of the flames was through my bedroom window.

The window in my bedroom was on the second floor at the rear of the house. It faced the driveway, which ran for a block between the backs of two rows of row-houses. There was a good chance I could survive a jump from the second floor. However, the window was directly over the steep, down-sloping entrance to our garage, which was under the house. That meant the extra height from the garage entrance made the jump from my window three floors high, not two. My survival from that extra height presented a real life and death problem that demanded I come up with a creative solution.

Over the next few days, I marshaled all my drawing and arithmetic skills to try and crack the problem. One of my better plans involved pillows. I decided I could tie them around my body, starting at my feet. When I was all covered with pillows, I'd waddle to the window and roll out. This plan depended on my being saved by the pillows.

One night mom was at neighbor's playing *Mahjong*, so I decided to try a dry run of my idea. All of it except the actual jump of course. I used couch pillows from the living room since they were large, firm, and very thick, not squishy like my bed pillows. I was able to cover everything but my arms, since I needed them to arrange the pillows in the right position and tie them, using the clothesline in the basement where mom hung the wash when bad weather made that necessary.

Finally, I finished wrapping and tying myself in the couch pillows. But I needed to see myself to make sure I was properly covered. There was a mirror over my little desk, next to my bed. But I could only see all of me if I used the bed like a trampoline. All I had to do was jump up and down until I was high enough to be level with the mirror, and in that way, get a glimpse of the whole me.

I must have looked like a gigantic hot dog bun with my head and shoulders sticking out one end of the pillows and my legs, sticking out from the other.

So, there I was, bouncing up and down like a mad man, over, and over and not quite making it high enough to get a good look.

After what seemed about forever, jumping with all the heavy pillows, I realized my balance, which wasn't that red hot to begin with, wasn't getting any better and on the last jump I can recall,

I missed the bed altogether. I guess I wacked myself pretty good because the next thing I knew, mom was there, putting a wet cloth on my forehead. I must have looked sort of weird, what with the pillows and ropes tied all around me. She wasn't mad—very sympathetic, as a matter of fact.

She just wanted to know, "What on earth were you doing wrapped up in pillows like that?

"Rehearsing for Halloween," I improvised. "I want to go as a couch." She was my mom, so she believed me.

Back then we lived on Cedar Park Avenue in North Philadelphia, which wasn't an avenue at all. And there sure as hell was no park. As for the trees—what's a kid know from trees? They had leaves and thick bark that could be pulled off in different size pieces.

One day I got this idea for how the tree in front of my house could be used to pass secret messages—just in case we came across any Nazi activity. So, let's say I wanted to leave a message for Worm (aka Seymour) or Wings (aka Jerry). I'd pull a large hunk of bark off the tree and using my Lone Ranger penknife, scoop out an opening big enough to hold a folded paper message. Then carefully fit the bark back over the hole like a puzzle piece. I'd then rush to Worm's house or call him on our phone—not the most secure way to deal with Nazi funny stuff, since our phone had a "party line" and I never knew who might be listening. Then Worm would go to the tree and retrieve the message.

I soon realized our plan had a few flaws. First of all, if I had to go to his house to tell him that the secret message was in the tree, why couldn't I just hand him the message, in person? Secondly, because we rarely could find the right piece of bark used to cover the message, the sender—in this case, me--would have to go with Worm or Wings and point out the right piece of bark—if, that is, the sender (aka me) could even find it again. I quickly learned all bark pieces look alike. And stripping the tree of all its bark just to find some dumb message seemed a bit extreme.

I really hated doing the message in the tree thing. I always felt like I was hurting the tree. Operating on it while it was awake and could feel the pain. Besides, it was probably the dumbest way on earth to pass secret messages.

A ritual of Summer in Philadelphia was the annual painting of the house numbers. It was usually in June, when a couple of guys, scruffy looking and reeking of alcohol, would show up and paint white oblongs on the curbs in front of each of the connected row houses on both sides of Cedar Park Avenue. They used a stencil, so each oblong was the same size, about a foot long and maybe five or six inches tall. It would take them almost a whole day to do our street—including cigarette and booze breaks and general horsing around. A day or so later, when the white oblongs were good and dry, they'd be back with number stencils, which they'd use to paint black numbers showing the address for each of the houses, on both sides of the street.

They did this once a year in front of every house in Philadelphia. However, if just once the mayor, or some other government hot-shot ever had to find a house number, while cars were parked solid, blocking the carefully painted black stenciled numbers, that would put an end to that little bureaucratic boondoggle.

UNCLE WALT

In those days, our dairy products were delivered by a "Milkman," dressed top to bottom in white: pants, shirt socks and shoes. Even a white, military style peaked cap. A black leather bow tie and black peak on his hat made him very official looking.

His stock of dairy products filled a large, white wagon, open on two sides. The wagon was pulled ever so slowly, by a huge work horse, and the wagon, the milkman and even the horse, were draped in a miasma of sour milk and manure.

The milkman would go from door to door and back and forth to the wagon, to make his deliveries and retrieve the empty glass bottles and jars. The clinking sounds as the various containers rattled against the wire basket carrier had a Pavlovian effect that brought out those housewives who needed to explain any out of the ordinary requests or comments for the next day's delivery.

"One extra sour cream, please."

"No chocolate milk tomorrow."

"Two bottles pasteurized milk every day next week. In laws coming."

"Returning cottage cheese from yesterday. I think it's bad. Please replace."

If my mom came to the door, our milkman always asked about my Uncle Walt. He knew Walt liked cottage cheese and occasionally would give us some, free.

"Give this to your brother," he would say. "And thank him from me for his service."

UNCLE WALT

These were the years during WWII, a time of radio, Saturday movies, and tearful separations. So many relatives, friends and neighbors suddenly gone. And then, seemingly like minutes later, back on leave, in uniform and then shipping overseas.

Polio was an annual epidemic. Food and gasoline and a bunch of other stuff was rationed, and everyone quickly learned how many "ration stamps" it took to buy whatever.

Although it was a long time ago, my memories of those early years are as vivid to me as the faces of my now grown children.

What does Uncle Walt have to do with all this?

Maybe nothing, but possibly everything.

I was half-way into my first year of high school in Philadelphia when pops took a job in a small town about fifty miles North of Philadelphia.

Pops sold our little house where I had lived most of my young life and we moved away.

Since our new home was a two-bedroom apartment with no usable basement or attic for Uncle Walt, he went to live in New Jersey with a distant relative of mom's.

Unlike when he left for war, a dozen years earlier, this time I didn't cry.

By the time I graduated from high school, we were several years into the Korean war. The media called it, "A Conflict," but it was a war all right and kids like me were being drafted and killed.

I could have enrolled in college and waited to be drafted or joined the National Guard or enlisted in the Army for a two-year hitch. But thanks to, or maybe because of Uncle Walt, I opted for the Air Force, which required a four-year commitment.

Seven years later and on my second four-year tour of duty, I was in Afghanistan when the call came that my Uncle Walt had died. By the time I was back in the states and could visit his grave, I had just started my ninth year in service and gotten my Staff Sergeant's stripes. I also had a lovely wife, Rita, who taught history at my former high school, and a beautiful seven-year-old little boy. We named him Walt, of course, but called him LW from the beginning, and still do.

Uncle Walt always said he wanted to be buried in the Philadelphia National Cemetery. So, when I finally got to visit his grave, I took LW with me. Since the cemetery was very near my old house on Cedar Park Avenue, it gave me a chance to show LW where his dad had grown up.

Cedar Park Avenue hadn't changed much. It did look a bit more prosperous than it had been when I lived there. The house numbers were still painted on the curbs. The trees were much larger but still had the thick bark I remembered so well. I couldn't help but wonder if a few of the pieces had grown over, and still covered a few of our secret messages.

Except for the trees, most everything looked smaller than I remembered. Part of that was because I was now 6'1". So, I assume that from LW's perspective it looked the same as it did to me when I was his age.

We walked around the old neighborhood for a while so I could point out some of the things I remembered: where I played stick ball, and a bunch of other games. The pharmacy where I bought Walt's Sir

Walter tobacco was now a soft-serve ice cream parlor. The houses where Wings and Worm had lived were still there, even though they were long gone. About a year ago I received a postcard from Worm. It had followed me, forwarded around the world, to every base where I had served, finally arriving during a dusty mail call in a green zone in Iraq. It was short, and to the point: Wings had been killed in a car crash and Worm was married and living in California, selling real estate.

Finally, LW and I climbed the steps of my old house and knocked on the front door. I stood there, somewhat nervous, looking sharp in my camo uniform, pants bloused over sand-colored boots, my beret adjusted to a regulation angle. LW was moving around and clearly had to use a bathroom.

After a few moments, an attractive African American teenager answered.

I introduced myself and LW and told her how I had lived in this very house and could I possibly do a walk through and show it to my son.

"I'm sure it'll be okay but just let me check with my dad," she said.

A moment later she was back and behind her was a tall man. From the resemblance, obviously the girl's father. He introduced himself as George Abbott.

I told him my story and he couldn't have been more gracious. We first took care of LW's bathroom needs. While waiting for him, George and I talked about the house.

"We've only lived here for a few years," he said. "The folks we bought it from retired and moved somewhere out West. Like Arizona or maybe it was New Mexico.

Shoshana, the daughter's name, called to her mother who came in and introduced herself. Helen was very chatty and said I could, of course, look around the house as much as I'd like.

The attic is what I was most interested in seeing. Would there be any remnants of Uncle Walt? Even just a faint whiff of Sir Walter Raleigh tobacco? But there was none.

I told the Abbotts of my uncle living in the attic. To my surprise, they had heard a few stories about Walter from a woman who grew up in the neighborhood and remembered there had been several veterans who lived on the block after the war.

George, his wife, Helen and I had been chatting in the living room for about a half hour. Shoshana was showing LW how to tie knots, since she was learning herself for a Girl Scout project.

Suddenly George snapped his fingers, "Damn," he said, half to himself, "I nearly forgot." He jumped up and left the room without explaining.

Helen and I just looked at each other, both bewildered.

"Sorry I took so long. It was in the cellar," George said, coming back into the room. "I knew it was inside one of those cartons we have down there. Just didn't know which one. When we bought the house, the owners gave us this. Said they got it from the folks who lived here before them. It belonged to someone who was here back in the forties. Personal stuff. No one, including us, wanted to throw it away. Figured someday somebody'd show up to claim it. Maybe that's you? Check it out, Sergeant. It just might have belonged to your Uncle Walt?"

I instantly recognized what George was holding. My hands shook as I reached out to take it.

UNCLE WALT

After lunch, we walked to Uncle Walt's grave site. We sat on the closely cropped, sun-warmed grass, the contents of my old cigar box spread out in front of us.

All of Walt's wartime notes to me are there. And much more. Walt's Purple Heart, Bronze Star and Air Medal. Each in its own presentation box. Some faded pictures of Walt in his uniform. Another of him next to the ball turret of his B-17 in full flying gear, either ready to take off, or just returning from a mission.

LW is fascinated by one of me and Walt. I recalled it was taken just before he left for England. He's in uniform and squatted down next to me. My arm is around his shoulder and I'm wearing his large, peaked cap, which on me, comes down around my ears.

And, to my surprise, there are several of his pipes and an empty Sir Walter Raleigh tobacco can. I open it and think I can still, just barely, get a whiff of its former contents.

Finally, we repack the cigar box. As we're leaving, I carefully place the Sir Walter Raleigh tobacco can on top of the pristine white gravestone.

And as we're walking away, I swear I can hear Walt, me and Wings coughing like crazy and shouting in unison,

"...let him out, because he's suffocatin' in there."

VIII
NORMAN NIPPLE AND THE DESK FROM HELL

A true story as told to me in a Tijuana biker bar

NORMAN NIPPLE AND THE DESK FROM HELL

It was Norman Nipple's first day on the job. He was very excited, and truth be told, a bit nervous.

Really Big Stuff, Inc. was the company where many people wanted to work. They paid higher wages than any other company in the valley and provided excellent health insurance, paid pregnancy leave—regardless of parental gender—generous vacation benefits and free donuts on Friday.

Norman's boss, Dingby Acton III was showing him the ropes and giving his new employee as much important information about Really Big Stuff as possible.

They also had an unspoken—and possibly illegal—penchant for hiring a preponderance of female personnel. Each tended to be attractive, and all seemed to be endowed with large breasts. A visual prerequisite enjoyed by all the men and—to be candid—more than a few of the women, as well.

Dingby whispered this last salacious tidbit immediately after a breast-distracted Norman Nipple accidentally smacked into the side of a desk.

RBSi's headquarter building was the size of several football fields.

It consisted of two floors. The top being for large, professionally decorated executive offices and a half-dozen elaborately appointed conference rooms. The ground floor was completely open space and about as attractive as a badly cluttered attic.

Row after row of identical wood desks and file cabinets covered most of the floor. Without the jumble of office paraphernalia it would have made a great aircraft hangar, which according to company lore, is how it served during the second world war.

Dingby Acton III and Norman stopped in front of one of the desks.

"I'd like you to meet Miss Nancy Zetter," Dingby said, placing his hand on Miss Zetter's back in what Norman thought was a strangely intimate gesture. "Miss Zetter is in Thread Counts," Dingby said, with great enthusiasm.

Norman gave a puzzled look as he "Helloed" Miss Zetter and pondered what it meant to be in Thread Counts.

Dingby III reading Norman's questioning expression said, "You see, RBS,"—using the short form for Really Big Stuff, Inc, which apparently only the top executives could use—"Really Big, to simplify things classifies each job by the clients the employee works with. And, so Norman, if you were paying attention, you'll know that Miss Zetter is in…?"

Norman was new here but it wasn't his first rodeo. "Miss Zetter is in *Thread Counts*."

Norman could see how well that went over with Dingby and being quick of wit, immediately followed up with. "And what will I be doing, sir?"

Dingby Acton III took Norman's arm in a surprisingly weak grip and guided him away from Miss Zetter's cluttered desk. In a tone of voice more appropriate for passing state secrets, he spoke, Norman noted, without seeming to move his lips, "You will be in *Paperclip Innovation.* It's not the most exciting right now but from projections I've seen, they have exciting plans in the paperclip pipeline that are clearly a road map to more and better."

Norman tried not to look as disappointed as he felt. Rather, he concentrated on the giant breasts of the woman seated at a desk they were passing.

Norman's first few months at Really Big Stuff, Inc. were uneventful. He quickly became popular—primarily because he didn't throw a fit whenever his carefully marked lunch bag was stolen from the refrigerator in the break room. It really didn't bother him since he preferred watching the bevy of breasts over a bowl of soup in the company cafeteria.

It was a Friday evening. Norman had been working late trying to empty his IN box before the long holiday weekend.

No one was around when Norman Nipple's desk first spoke to him.

"How are you Norman?" a sultry woman's voice cooed softly.

Norman damn near shit his pants.

"*What the fuck!*" was about all he could muster as he looked around and under everything near and not so near his desk.

"Don't be afraid, Norman," the pleasant-sounding voice continued. "I'm right here."

Norman proceeded to open all the drawers in his desk and looked in and under the IN and OUT boxes.

"No, Normy, I am your desk. I only want some company. I'm very lonely. And a little horny, too, if truth be told. A woman has needs, you know."

"Horny? *You're a little HORNY?!* You're just a desk, for crying out loud. There's no such things as horny desks. It would be like…

like a—I don't know…maybe gay staplers? Or bisexual typewriters? A…"

"Okay, I get your point, Normy. You don't mind if I call you Normy, do you? You remind me of a boss I had on another job. He was a Normy, too and you could be his stunt double."

"Look, er, ah, Miss Desk, I know you're not real. Just a figment in my head—a concoction, fabrication, hallucination, illusion, delusion, mirage, apparition, a chimera..."

"Oh, Normy, you're so narrow-minded. I can be a woman, too, if I want. Females are great at multi-tasking, you know," she said, her middle drawer pouting. "Don't believe me? Place your hand on my top right drawer."

Norman sighed, resigned that he'd had a major stroke or a brain bleed of some kind. He tried to recall if his RBSi insurance covered disability. He reached over to touch the upper right drawer.

His hand shot back as if he'd been electric-shocked. "Oh my God! It feels like naked flesh. Like a breast or something."

"I told you. Nice, isn't it? Just like a breast. Wait until I show you how to stroke my center drawer keyhole," the voice said in a fair imitation of Dolly Parton.

"By the way, my name is L'ived. But it's pronounced any way you wish.

Norman was backing away from his desk. "Listen, whatever your name is, I must be going. I need major medical attention. You're nothing more than a symptom of my brain doing back flips. If I'm not back here next week you'll know I didn't pull through. So hope for a nice replacement."

Norman's visit to the Emergency Room at Our Lady of Misbehavior General Hospital proved to be a waste of time. Consensus was, he'd had a panic attack. He left the ER with a vial of strong pills for anxiety and the recommendation he take a long vacation.

Most of Norman's long weekend was a drugged blur. He popped pills, ate pizza and thought about the "feel" of the top, right-hand drawer of his desk. And of What's-her-name.

On Monday morning Norman Nipple was feeling much better, convinced he'd had a panic attack and ready to dive into the complex world of paperclip work.

Pondering Friday, Norman marveled at how much stress and anxiety had fucked up his head. He had to keep reminding himself that paperclip development was not brain surgery.

Smiling, he slid in behind his desk and tossed out a friendly, "Hello," to Billy Batson, the man at the desk to Norman's left. Billy was in *Victorian Molding* and, without looking up, nodded back to Norman in response.

"How was your weekend?" whispered L'ived in her low, sexy voice.

Norman looked over at Billy Batson, "You say something, Billy?"

Billy put his hand over the mic on his head set and whispered, "Sorry Norman, I'm on a sales call."

"No, Normy, it's me. How was your weekend? Did you get a clean bill of health? I was thinking maybe you could stay late tonight, have dinner here and I could show you some of the more interesting parts of my construction."

That's when Norman gasped, clutching his chest and slowly slid to the floor. As he lay dying on the cool faux hardwood his life did not pass in front of him. But her name did. It was in huge, white letters and sat on a rolling hill like the HOLLYWOOD sign. And before it all turned to black, he realized what *L'ived* spelled when his mind's eye saw it backwards.

Norman Nipple's funeral took place the following week. The only RBSi person in attendance was Dingby Acton III.

The following week, in Norman's place was an attractive woman. Well endowed, of course. Before she left for the day, from the knee hole of Norman's former desk came a sexy, deep male voice that whispered, "Hi, beautiful, my name is L'ived. It's French. Have you ever made love on a desk, with a desk?"

STORY IX
A COOKIE FOR POP

A COOKIE FOR POP

My pop is a small man with a large, impacted sweet tooth.

A handful of last year's Halloween candy corn? A slice of seven-layer cake? If its sweet, Pop is happy.

He's also a junk-food junkie.

Pop recently turned seventy-five and is, as he puts it, *horse healthy.* His doctors say he likely gets his longevity from his father, Moe, who lived to a ripe ninety-three. Growing up, I don't recall my grandfather ever being sick. And his diet—if it could be called a diet—consisted of whatever my grandmother put down in front of him three times a day.

My doctor says I may have inherited what he calls designer genes.

But honestly, I think whatever longevity I may enjoy is thanks to my wife, Julia. She guards my nutritional landscape with the intensity of a junkyard pit bull.

As a result, the protective gastronomical guard-rails she's built around us contain lots of roughage and low fat. Sweet comes from fruit. No refined anything. No processed anything. Organic everything.

I know you're thinking that it's worth the effort. But, trust me, there are times when it's a total pain in the ass. Especially, when Mom and Pop come for dinner.

When eating at our place, he's unhappy. At their place, we're unhappy.

We were not always this picky about food.

A COOKIE FOR POP

Julia and I first met on a Saturday morning, as we attempted to pass each other in one of Fairway Market's crushingly narrow aisles. A quick glance at the content of each other's baskets, and it was love at first sight.

We both had loads of salty/greasy snacks. Smoked fish. Bags of bagels. Full fat yogurt and plastic containers with a variety of olives—hers were manzanillas and mine, the kalamatas I loved, especially when one was at the bottom of a Vodka martini.

But what caught my eye was the variety of cheese she had. I love cheese and it was clear, so did Julia. And we each had a long *ficelle* sticking up from our basket like a carbohydrate antenna.

As it turned out, we lived a few blocks apart on Riverside drive. Even though it was a short walk from the market to Julia's place, it was enough time to discover we had a mutual friend, Sam Feder.

We got to Julia's building first. She took out her phone, excused herself and walked a few steps away to make a call. When she finished, she came back and invited me for lunch.

Of course, I accepted.

I rushed to my apartment, dumped the groceries and brushed my teeth. On the way out, I grabbed my cheese purchases and a bottle of wine and returned to Julia's apartment.

While she set the table and put out the various cheeses, I opened the bottle of 1984 Jordan Cabernet I had been saving for such an occasion. I poured it immediately to give it time to breathe and unwrapped the meter-long crusty *ficelle.*

Between the two of us, we must have bought $50 worth of

cheese —much more in today's dollars. We didn't eat it all but we made quite a dent in our stash. We finished the Jordan Cabernet and ate the bread down to the last crumb.

That's when Julia told me she called Feder to check me out.

She said, "I wasn't going to invite you to lunch if you were a serial killer or just unhappily married and horny."

Julia and I quickly became an item.

And going to the market every Saturday became our special ritual. With the help of the store's cheese monger, Steve, we tasted our way into the complex world of *fromage.*

Goat cheese was our favorite, yet there were others, as well.

There is a lovely little cheese that comes from Corsica called *Brin d' Amour*, which means sprig of love. It has, to me, the wonderful flavor of a fine aged Muenster.

We also enjoyed very old Gouda. When it gets to be about five years of age it takes on a hard, crunch consistency.

And, of course, we would drop a small fortune on the chèvres. One of our favorites is a New York State Bicorne covered with garlic and herbs. And a *Bouton De Coulotte Maconnais* warmed in a toaster oven, it's perfect when plopped in the middle of a green salad.

Without fail, a *Clochette Berry* will find its way into our shopping cart. It's a wonderful mild chèvre shaped like a bell that has a pleasant, tangy tartness.

Then there is the herb covered, creamy goat cheese called *Perigord carré*. And the delightful Mole Hill chèvre dubbed *Taupinière.*

When we had an especially nice bottle of white wine, we would be sure to get a *St. Christophe en Bazelle.* It's a chèvre molded on a stick like a lollypop, then covered with milk ash. Or the other milk-ash-encased-goat called *Épigny*. White paper covers over the ash that makes it look like icing on a cake.

A COOKIE FOR POP

Julia and I had been living together for almost two years when I was offered an excellent job in Dallas, Texas. Being entrenched New Yorkers, Dallas wasn't a place we were excited about, but the opportunity was just too good to turn down.

We'd been living in Dallas for almost six months when I sent first class tickets to my folks to come visit.

As my parents were going to be with us for two weeks, the issue of food was bound to be a point of contention. An occasional dinner with them in New York was tolerable, but three meals a day for fourteen days was another cup of prune juice.

Julia does a pretty good job of sticking to our diet regimen, even if 'healthy' food shopping in Dallas is more akin to a scavenger hunt.

After all, Dallas is the home of the Chicken Fried Steak. And there are more barbecue joints, it seems, than Stetsons. The "Healthy Food" section of our supermarket is roughly the size of a small car port. If Cardiologists gave an award for The Clogged Artery State of The Year, the Lone Star would win, hands down. With my parents in situ for two weeks, our healthy diet will drop Pop into one of the lower rings of Victual Hell.

We were standing in the kitchen while Mom and Pop unpacked in the spare room.

"God knows what junk food your father has packed in his luggage," Julia whispers. "When they went to your sister's, she told me he had Mounds-bars, Ring Dings and Devil Dogs hidden inside his shoes," Julia said.

"My sister's a drama queen. He didn't have any candy bars. It was one large bag of dark chocolate chips. No big deal. Anyway, I thought dark chocolate is supposed to be good for you."

The following morning Julia whipped up omelets for breakfast. She only uses the egg whites, which drives Pop crazy.

"What are you doing with the yolks?" he says with alarm. "You're wasting the best part." I can almost hear his dentures clenching with frustration.

When I was working, Julia entertained my folks, driving them around the area, seeing the sights and exposing them to fresh air. The outings included the food shopping necessary every day or so.

One evening Pop had us all falling on the floor from laughter, as he recounted how Julia picked out the food. "She examines everything," he said. "If it's in a can or a box, she reads it. If it's not, she smells it. Yesterday she was smelling chicken butts. She even checks fish eyes. I swear she turned down a branzino, claiming it had an astigmatism."

Even Julia had to laugh at that.

The last week in November found us all together on the twenty-second floor of our highrise apartment. Texans call them skyrises. I—along with Mom and Pop—sat in the living room examining the Dallas skyline. An impressive array of healthy appetizers filled most of the coffee table. Julia was in the kitchen putting the final touches on dinner.

I could see that Pop was in a muddle as he examined the spread Julia had laid out. He was trying to find anything he thought looked the least bit edible. There were peapods and a nice dip. A dozen little squares of baked tofu on toothpicks. A mango spread on no-salt rice crackers. And Julia's special. Grape leaves wrapped around a mixture of cottage cheese and strawberry preserves.

In truth, there are sweets in the apartment. A half dozen big, fat sugar cookies that we brought with us from New York sit in the fridge door rack between a jar of hot mustard, and another of cornichon. The cookies are in a bag, which at one time held coffee beans. The type of bag that rolls down as the coffee is used and seals with little fold-back tabs, so the contents stay fresh.

We had gotten the sugar cookies from a friend in New York as a going-away present. You may think a bag of cookies is a punk gift. But these cookies happen to contain about a half ounce of King Cobra, a powerful, super fine weed.

Our friend, Tracy, had gotten the cookies from her dealer, Star—who resides in Portland, Oregon. Star is one of those over-the-hill hippies who sold weed and mushrooms to support herself in the late 60s and 70s. In 1973, Oregon became the first State to decriminalize cannabis. Star's business exploded. From the narrow bounds of a hippie clientele Star was now running a very lucrative and far-ranging business.

When selling weed became a low-margin commodity, Star determined there was more to be made converting the weed into very profitable edibles. So, she became a baker, converting all sorts of cookies, and pastries—each serving as an aspic for excellent marijuana.

The quality and inherent potency of her product is above reproach. I can attest to the claim of their potency—Julia and I having gotten smashed on just a small piece of one of her products.

So, we save the cookies we have for very, very special occasions.

A COOKIE FOR POP

Near the end of my parents' two-week visit, Julia and I needed a break and decided take in a movie. I believe my parents were happy to have some alone time, as well.

I love my parents but still, it was a relief to be alone, just the two of us, by ourselves. After the film, we dropped into a restaurant we like. We sat at the bar and, feeling euphoric—a bit like escaped convicts—we broke our own rules and ordered martinis and burgers.

By the time we got back to the apartment we expected to find my parents fast asleep.

We entered the apartment like parents, not children—slow and quiet—not wanting to wake up the "kids."

The living room was in semi-darkness. A mini-spot illuminated a five-foot African sculpture. The ambient glow of nighttime Dallas came through the glass sliding doors that ran across one long wall of the room.

I walked into the kitchen and flipped on the light.

Our apartment is always spotless. If anything is out of place, we know it. It's kind of a sixth sense. Luckily, Julia and I share this compulsion, or we'd drive each other insane. Or worse.

The kitchen is a shocking disaster. A huge pizza box lay open on the sink. The dregs of what had been a large-with-everything pie, was next to two open wine bottles. One empty and the other half full, the latter, on its side. Some had spilled on the counter and had dripped onto the floor. The leftover turkey from last night's dinner is stripped to the bare bones. Dirty dishes and utensils scattered about.

We looked at each other but said nothing. There wasn't much we could say. It was obvious my mature parents—never more than social drinkers—had visited our wine rack, which led to an eating spree, the results of which spread out in front of us.

I left the kitchen and went to their room. I could hear the

television and tapped on the door. No answer. I knocked again a bit louder. Still no response. I opened the door and entered. The bed is empty, still carefully made from this morning. I imagined a scene in the bathroom. Pop kneeling over the toilet puking his guts out and my mother holding a wet cloth to his forehead. But the bathroom was empty, too.

The apartment is not that big and we quickly searched every inch of it. Even opening closets and drawers.

We rapidly moved from concerned to frantic. I was about to call the police when Mom and Pop drifted in through one of the sliding glass doors that led to the balcony.

My pop, noticeably swaying said, his speech slurred, "We were in the pouch." My mother, obviously DUI (without a car) added, "We fell asheep. Those loungers are very—you know—loungy. Sheepy Time for bed now." And then she giggled.

I was speechless and could only stare at them. They looked disheveled and my mother had a red wine stain on her white blouse. I couldn't scold them, they were my parents. And it wasn't their fault we couldn't find them. We neglected to look on the balcony. So I resorted to sarcasm.

"You want something more to eat before you go to bed?" After a pizza and a turkey you must still feel a bit peckish."

My father actually thought about it. "I could go for some Zabar's chocolate babka," and then he started laughing. Mom joined in and they kept right on laughing as they staggered down the hall to their room.

As Julia and I began cleaning up the mess, we could hear them laughing for another fifteen or twenty minutes.

The evening was never mentioned again. A few days later they left to return to New York. Regardless of the "event," as it became known, it was a wonderful visit. One of the best I've had alone with my parents since I was a kid. In later years, after my parents' passing, the "event" became one of those classic family stories, told over and over again.

It was several months since Mom and Pop's visit and both Julia and I had had a rough week. She recently started a job she hated and things at my office were not going well. I doubted we would still be in Dallas this time, next year.

It seemed the perfect time to get a little blasted. Julia went to take a shower and I went to get a half of one of the drug-laden cookies. A half of one of them would be more than enough for us both.

Even as I reached for the coffee bean package, I sensed it would be empty. I opened it anyway.

All I found inside was a note in my father's hand. At least it looked like his writing, yet a tad erratic. The message was simple: *"You've been holding out on us son. Buy more of these. They're delicious. See if they come in oatmeal."*

All I could do was laugh and mix a shaker of martinis.

The next day I contacted our friend Tracy and she contacted her friend in Portland and, don't you know, they do come in oatmeal. So we arranged to get a half-dozen every month or so delivered to Mom and Dad.

My parents have never seemed happier. They brought a brand-new cassette player and we've sent them all our Beetles tapes.

My mom lost weight and is jogging a few miles every day.

And Pop has grown a beard.

STORY X
A REALLY GREAT FUNERAL

A REALLY GREAT FUNERAL

Life has been good to Max Rifkin. He has a loving wife, Rose, a decent job as the Chief Operating Officer of a small successful business. The mortgage on their Upper Westside Co-op is almost paid off. Their only child, Max, Jr., is married and living in California where he owns a highly successful theatrical agency.

For the past few years, Max and Rose have been carefully planning for Max's eventual retirement. High on the their list of possibilities is a "coin-toss" between Worldwide travel or touring America in one of those fancy Recreational Vehicles. They spend many pleasant hours together pouring over maps and travel brochures. But, sadly, a year before Max was to retire, Rose dies. Grief stricken, Max retires. Soon several of his closest friends move to warmer climes, and Max, suddenly finds himself virtually alone.

Eight Months Later

For some time, Max, Jr., has insisted that his father relocate to Los Angeles to be with him, his bitch-of-a- wife, Bonnie and Max's obnoxious eight-year-old grandson, Henry.

Max, a lifelong New Yorker, under extreme pressure from his son, finally capitulates and moves to the West Coast.

A REALLY GREAT FUNERAL

Home for Max is now in Westwood, a lovely, very affluent community bordering Beverly Hills. The entire space over his son's three-car garage has been comfortably rebuilt into a compact one-bedroom apartment. Even Max must admit, he's got a pretty good set up. His little place is not only free, but is also maintained—including laundry—by his son's live-in housekeeper. Best of all, the apartment has its own entrance, so he can come and go as he pleases.

Once settled, Max joins a nearby health club. The Apex.

Max, a personable and extroverted guy, is easily absorbed into a group of similarly aged male members. Most weekdays they show up to do their various and separate level and degree of exercise. Then, after that, take a steam or relax in the sauna, shower, shave and eventually gather for breakfast in Apex's small café.

Max's life quickly and easily falls into a fairly fixed routine. He peddles his bike every morning to the Apex—less than a mile away from his apartment. By the time his group finishes breakfast it's almost noon so Max spends the rest of the day reading, walking around Westwood, taking in a movie and, on occasion, hire an Uber to take him to spend an afternoon in one of Los Angeles's many museums.

Every so often, he and Max, Jr., would take a pleasant 4-hour drive to Las Vegas, to take in a few shows and gamble. Young Max, Jr., loved to gamble and was known, especially at the Bellagio Hotel and Casino, as a *whale*—the gambling industry's argot for a very *high roller*—one who bets large amounts of money.

After a dozen or so trips to Las Vegas with his son, Max became well known to the managers at the Bellagio and is afforded some of the same deferential treatment as his *high roller* son.

It was one of those raw and cold L.A. mornings that are so unusual in Southern California. Max, in deep depression, peddled to the Apex and went right to the steam room. He sat wrapped in towels for as long as he could stand it. Once showered and dressed he drifted into the cafe and was greeted warmly by his buddies. Handshakes and hugs were accompanied with cracks about his recent few days spent in Las Vegas—most, along the line of, *Did you get laid? How were the shows? How much did you win?*

Finally settling in, he half-listened to their familiar and predictable banter as he slowly surveyed the diverse bunch of old guys who'd become his friends. They'd all gravitated to California from here-and-there, at various times, and for various reasons; drawn, like metal shavings, to a strong magnet.

It was a good bet that in their former lives they'd have found little, if anything, in common. But advanced age, retirement, and a certain amount of loneliness, had leveled the playing field. So now, here they were... *just a few old guys*, each with his unique history, talent, temperament, and individual quirkiness.

Max tries to listen, to pay some attention to his friends' words. But all he can think about are his last twenty-four hours in Las Vegas and the pile of shit he's in, right up to his slightly askew hairpiece. He must tell someone, just to get some of the pressure off his chest. But He doesn't know exactly how to broach the subject, but he desperately needs to get rid of it, expel it like a fishbone stuck in the back of his throat. The "boys" are the only ones he can confide in. If only Rose was still alive. She would know what to do.

Fuck it, just blurt it out.

"Guys…hello, I got a big problem."

A real big problem.

"I need some advice," Max said.

Since they were all tied up with their own rhetoric, shouting back and forth, they never heard a word Max said.

He tried it again.

"Listen, guys, shut up for a minute. I got a big problem."

A real big problem.

"I need your advice," Max said, this time his voice cracking slightly, adding to his profound level of seriousness.

And then he waited as the other voiced died down.

Arnold '*Noodles*' Handholder was the first to respond to Max. Handholder was a tall, skinny widower of seventy-eight years, and the former owner of *La Fong's*, a little Chinese noodle shop in downtown LA.

"What kind'a problem you got ," Noodles said, his voice curling into a question mark? "Like what is the nature of said problem?"

"*WHAT DID HE SAY?*" Sam Bend asked, inserting a finger into his ear, groping for the volume control on his hearing aid.

"*He said he got a problem,*" Noodles shouted.

Sam found the volume control and responded in a close-to-normal tone. "Christ, don't tell me you caught the clap? Can they find out so quick?"

Sam Bend had originally been Sam Benderwitz, back in his Chicago days, when he was in the printing business. But he was forced to fold his little company when his accountant took off with the firm's assets, which included Sam's wife. Sam changed his name for what he called, a *professional necessity*, since he now made a marginal living, out of his apartment, selling Catholic devotional items by mail order. It was an unusual product line, even for a 'sparsely' observant Jew.

"Let's hear what the fuck he has to say, you guys! Give him some breathing room," Rocco Cappelli said, forcefully. Rocco was a handsome man, short of stature, but long a liberal use of aftershave. His hair was thick and pure white, contrasting nicely with his swarthy, well-tanned coloration. His teeth were a dazzling testimony to the miracles of implantation, and easy credit.

Rocco hailed from what he referred to as, *Back East*, and took delight in hinting he just might have been a *'connected'* guy. Possibly to support that allusion, he always preferred seating with his back to a wall—with the entrance in plain sight. It might have been a ruse, however a car's backfire or a suddenly dropped tray of tableware had been known to levitate him several inches off a chair.

In response to Rocco's call to let Max speak, Howie Brechmeyer chimed in. "Is this a legal problem? Cause if it is, remember, I'm not licensed to practice in California, but I'm sure I can help."

Brechmeyer had been a hotshot divorce attorney in Manhattan who suddenly shuttered his practice when one of his clients—an attractive, and massively endowed porn star, aptly named, *Loretta LeBoff*—accused Howie of secretly photographing her while—as she so daintily put it—went to *powder her nose.*

When he passionately denied the accusation, *Ms. LeBoff* wordlessly countered by pushing aside his large, framed law diploma, revealing the one-way mirror between his office and the "powder" room.

Litigation was avoided when Howie wrote *Ms. LeBoff* an obscenely large check and walked away while he still had a few resources left to do so.

Retired, Howie now enjoyed the Apex health club, surfing the net, Tango, and adding to his already extensive collection of rare, as well as everyday raunchy pornography.

Howie only dated divorced women with large breasts and a drinking habit. It was a strategic choice—not unlike, he claimed, a lion going after the weakest wildebeest in a herd. He also expected his '*quarry*'—after several dates, of course—to wear one of the Girl Scout outfits he kept, in various sizes, in his bedroom closet.

So, what's the problem?" Howie said, folding his Wall Street Journal, and removing his reading specks.

Max looked sheepishly around the table. "I had, uh, a little trouble in Vegas."

"Yeah, you said, but not to worry," laughed Noodles, "we got your back, right guys? Long as it's not about money or sex."

"No, Noodles, I'm serious…something really…*bad* happened," Max said.

"Don't tell me you picked up something," Howie said.

"Shut up and let him talk!" Sam Bend yelled, assuming everyone's hearing was as bad as his own.

"Trust me, a case of the clap would have been a gift, next to what happened," Max said, bitterly.

"Yeah, so what happened, already?" Noodles said.

"You know how I like to shoot craps?" With nods and shrugs, the groups agreed. "Well, I was doing okay, you know? Having a nice little run…actually, a fantastic run."

"The only fantastic run you have is when you make it out of bed in the middle of the night to take a pee," Howie said.

"If he's *LUCKY*, he's makes it out of the bed!"

"Please, guys?" Max was silent for a moment, trying to gather is thoughts. "So, like I was saying…I was doing okay. But then, I started losing."

"Schmuck, in the end you always lose," Noodles said, only the house wins.

"Seriously, Noodles. I lost a bundle."

"Yeah? So what's a bundle hotshot?" Noodles inquired with a chuckle.

Max looked a bit sheepish. "Twenty-eight thousand dollars," he said, barely over a whisper.

"*WHAD' YOU SAY? YOU LOST HOW MUCH?*" Sam yelled, his finger probing his ear for the volume control.

"*Jesus…H…Christ, Max! You lost TWENTY EIGHT GRAND?*" Rocco said with a tone of awe in his voice. "Where the name of hell'd you get that kind of scratch?"

"That's my point exactly! *I didn't have the money. It's where* I got it, is the problem. I must have been out of my mind. Momentarily insane! I really screwed up. I don't know what I'm going to do," Max said, burying his face in his hands.

"Max, listen to me…without money, how could you ever get in that deep?" Howie asked, reaching out and touching his shoulder.

Max looked up, pulling himself together. "Slowly. I started off with a few hundred of my own Max, Jr., gave me another thousand in chips. I built it up to a few large. Then he got a call from his office and had to go back. We had tickets for a show so I stayed. Getting back by bus was no problem.

"So I kept playing. I won a few more thousand."

"See, that's when you walk away," Howie said.

"Then I started to lose."

"Yeah, so, you lost. Then what? You got a visit from the cash fairy?" Noodles said.

"No, well sort of. But that's when I really fucked up. You know how Max, Jr., always sets me up to stay at the Bellagio? It's because he has a very large credit line there. Very, very large. He's considered a Whale. So when he walks in, they kiss his ass. I've seen it. Unbelievable! Anything he wants. Rooms, meals…whatever. And it's all free…the hotel comps everything. So, when I lost the thousand, I figured, hell, I can win it back…if I can just play…a little longer."

Noodles was silent, just shaking his head.

"You shoulda walked away," Rocco said.

"Yeah, your brilliant hindsight is noted," Max said, sarcastically. "Very astute. Anyway, I didn't know what to do. And then I got this idea. I went to the cashier's cage, showed the kid there my driver's license. She checks with the computer and, of course, up pops Max Rifkin—same name, same address. Of course, it's my son, Max Rifkin. But she don't know the difference. As far as the cute, blonde kid working the cage is concerned, I'm Max Rifkin, and that's all she needs to know. The account's flagged with a big VIP status on the screen, so she's ready to give me anything I ask for."

"She'd probably give you a blowjob if you wanted," Rocco said.

"Believe me, I would'a been better off. But instead, I take two large. I worked it up again, into five thousand! And then lost it. But I still felt I could get it all back. So I went for a couple more. This back and forth went on all night. By six the next morning, I'm half out of my mind and in the hole for *twenty-eight fucking grand!*"

"Shit, Max, won't your kid cover the marker for you?" Noodles said.

"Of course he could, but that's not the point. I don't even want him to know what happened. His bitch of a wife has been trying to convince him to put me into one of those assisted living joints somewhere. She's convinced I'm losing it just because she knows I can't stand her. Actually, hating her is probably one of my saner instincts."

"How did you get out of Vegas without, you know, paying something or signing some papers?" Sam shouted.

"I went to the manager and told him what happened—the mix up with the name, all the money…everything. I begged him for time to cover the loss, to get the money back to the Bellagio."

"Christ, the guy had to know the house fucked up big time. How could they just give out that kind of money without checking for the right Rifkin," Howie said in his best, disbarred tone-of-voice.

"I know. You're right. Luckily, he also knows my kid very well, so he gave me until the end of the month to pay it back, but after that, he said he'd have to contact Max, Jr.,"

"That's less than a month from now," Sam said.

"You do have some money, don't you? What about your investments," Howie asked.

"Ha," Max laughed sourly. "Bad timing's been the story of my life. A couple months ago Max Jr. had his financial advisors dump the proceeds from my New York apartment, plus what investments I had into an annuity. It gives me a nice, steady check every month, but there's no way I could pull twenty-eight thousand in cash out of it. Besides, the minute I tried to, they'd call my kid.

The five of them were silent. No one knew what to say or, for that matter, what to do. Twenty-Eight thousand dollars was a lot of money. Especially if you don't have it.

A REALLY GREAT FUNERAL

For the next few days Max, in deep depression, was a no-show at the club. The reason was clear to his friends, and they decided they'd better have an immediate intervention. Max agreed to a meeting. It was arranged for that night at Howie's apartment.

Even after copious amounts of Chinese take out, and a great deal of Vodka, they still couldn't come up with a solution to Max's financial catastrophe.

But rather than sit silently and stare at each other, they opted to watch the new porno Howie had just received from a fellow pervert in Sweden.

Five-minutes into a disgustingly erotic video, involving a nun, two choirboys and several ears of parish-grown corn, Noodles spoke up.

"Okay, Max…here's a wild thought. Rocco, you always *'implied'* you got connections, so why can't we get the bucks from one of your contacts Back East?

Rocco's mouth immediately popped into a wide grin. "Guys… you cannot believe how long I've waited to say this?" And then he stood and broke into a full-throated, Godfather growl: *"Just when I thought I was out…they pull me back in!"*

"Can you please cut the Al Pacino shit and just give me an answer," Noodles said, a stern edge creeping into his voice. "This is serious. Can you get the money, or not?"

Rocco slowly added ice to his Vodka before answering. "Yeah. Sure. I know people could arrange it. Only two little *prob-lem-o's.*"

"Yeah, and so…?"

"The *vig,*" Rocco explained—using the street slang for interest charges—"…the vig on a loan like that can be cruel."

"Oh, great. And what's the number two *prob-lem-o?* Cancer?"

"Worse than cancer. Paying them back the twenty-eight large

is the easy part. It's the vig, which could run, maybe, six, eight grand a month. And that's on top of the twenty-eight. Take your pick: Vegas with twenty-eight large or the mob with God-only-knows how much. Either way you're fucked."

"Okay, I understand!" Max shouted, "But, at least, if I can just pay the Bellagio, my kid won't know how stupid I was. I'd never forgive myself if he found out."

They all sat in silence once again, knowing they were back where they started.

Surprisingly, it was Sam Bend, of all people, who came up with a completely wacky *little* nugget that, in turn, triggered a workable *big* idea.

"I KNOW THIS WILL SOUND…"

"Turn it down, Sam, you're breaking my ear drums," Rocco said, cupping his ears with the palms of his hands.

"UH, SORRY," Sam said, adjusting his aid, and continuing several decibels softer. "This will sound like I had too much to drink Max, but what if there was a thing you could do that would make your son give up twenty-eight thousand dollars, without knowing it was you getting the money?"

"I'd say that would be right up there with the *'wine-into-water'* thing. Besides, how do you propose pulling off this little miracle? Tell him it's for Girl Scout cookies, or maybe, a UJA contribution?"

Sam sensed it was time for the *'coup de grace'* of his idea and, sensing he had the group's attention, sat a bit taller, "No. He'd, uh, give the money up as, uh, as a…a *RANSOM*!" Sam said, hesitantly.

"A *ransom*?" Max sputtered.

"Ransom for what?" Noodles said, making a face like he smelled something foul.

"Well, uh…to get his kid back," Sam said, simply.

For a long thirty-seconds there was total silence, as they all stared at Sam, like he was a train wreck.

Then, the room verbally exploded.

"A *RANSOM* for *my grandson*? My own fucking GRANDSON! That's the sickest fucking idea I ever heard!"

"But you don't even like him! You said so yourself he nothing but a snot nose kid," Sam countered, defensively.

"That's not the point, asshole," Max slapped back.

"You'd never get away with it," Howie's head-shook and, forgetting for a second, he no longer practiced law, reflexively groped for a non-existent business card. "It's…a Federal…fucking offense."

"Geez, Sam, what were you thinking? Snatch him from school at recess? Mail his old man one of his tiny fingers or an ear, or something? It's insane. Didn't you ever hear about the Lindbergh baby? We're talking FBI, death penalty kind of stuff, for God's sake!"

"If you say so," Sam pouted. "But I'd bet it could work."

Silence again. More Vodka shots poured all-around. And the five of them sat crumbling fortune cookie remains and pondering, or at least whatever passed for pondering.

Eventually, Howie broke the silence in a thinking-out-loud whisper.

"*Wait…one…fucking…minute.* What if we could do that, have a kidnapping…but one that wasn't *really* a kidnapping? You know what I mean?"

"No, I really don't have a fucking clue what you mean…and I think we'd better all have a time out. Get some coffee. We're starting to sound really nuts," Max, said.

"Hold on. I want to hear what Howie's thinking," Rocco injected.

"Okay, here's what I'm thinking," Howie said, standing for

greater emphasis. "Go back to what Sam said before. He may have been on to something."

"See, I told you it was a good idea," Sam said proudly.

"By all means, elaborate," Noodles said.

"Think about it. There is one person in the world Max can kidnap without actually, you know…actually kidnapping anybody… and would be worth twenty-eight thousand dollars to Max, Jr.,."

"Well, clearly this evening's porno has affected his brain," Rocco mumbled, to no one in particular.

"And who might this person be, that Max can snatch so freely?" Noodles asked.

"Obviously, it can't be the kid, Rocco said."

"Do they have a dog?"

"What kind of idiot pays twenty-eight grand for a dog?"

"Hey, wait! I'd put up a few Franklins for my Fredo," Rocco said with some indignation.

Noodles held his hand up. "Guys! Please…in fairness, let's hear Howie out."

"Thank you Noodles. Okay, in a nutshell, here it is—The one person who can be kidnapped, and who's important enough to have Max, Jr., part with twenty-eight big ones—and without actually snatching anyone, is…"

"WHO," they asked in unison?

"Max, of course," Howie said, proudly.

You could hear a pin drop.

Son of a bitch," Noodles whispered.

Over the following week the details of Howie's plan were debated, adopted, discarded, modified, altered, revised…and, finally, agreed upon.

The plan was as simple as it was stupidly naive. Max would simply walk out of the house, leaving a ransom note, along with a "proof of life plea" recorded on Max's own cell phone. He would then hole-up in Howie's spare room where if bored, he could while away the hours breast-stroking through Howie's sea of pornography. Once the ransom money arrived, he would return home, safe and none the worse for wear.

The details went onto a list that each man committed to memory. Or tried, at least, to commit to memory.

1. Max will re-record the "proof of life" message on his mobile phone, which, as instructed on the ransom note, will play when his own mobile number is called.

2. Howie will write the words for a ransom note, using his legal skills to make it vaguely specific.

3. Sam will construct the ransom note itself, using letters/words cut from various magazines. (Nothing from AARP publications. Potentially too obvious.)

4. Max will not leave the house until it's certain he will not be observed. When that time comes, Max will call Howie, making sure he's available to pick up Max. (If Howie is not available, the operation will be aborted.)

5. Before leaving the house, Max will place his mobile phone and the ransom note in the garage duct taped to the seat of his bicycle.

6. Max will leave garage lights on, and one of the automatic doors open—something that will surely alert his family to something suspicious.

7. Max will proceed to the southwest corner at the eastern end of his bock to await pick up by Howie.

8. Howie arrives and drives (staying within speed limit) to Howie's apartment.

All that remained was the 10th point—not actually on the list—and that was for Max's family to find the ransom note and follow its instructions to wait for the kidnappers to call on Max's mobile.

Once the ransom payment—in used, unmarked bills—is paid, Max will return, safe and sound to his family.

The Bellagio would get its money, and all will be right with the world.

Now all Max needs is the perfect day to kidnap himself.

On Thursday of the following week, Max was relieved and thrilled when his son informs him that the Friday night dinner previously planned, would not take place since he, along with the bitch and the churlish child, would be leaving for a few nights in San Diego; and would not return until late afternoon, on Sunday.

Sure enough, the next day, not long after the school bus spit-out Max's grandson, Henry, the family's car cleared the drive and is on its way. Max waits a few hours just in case they return for something forgotten. He then phones Howie and, using a code devised for the plan, says simply, *"Max-attack is go."*

A moment of hesitation, then the answer, *"Attack is a go, Roger,"* indicating Howie is okay to make the pick-up and will arrive in approximately ten minutes. Max follows his pre-rehearsed checklist carefully attaching the ransom note and mobile phone with duct tape onto the bike seat . A short time later, Max is at Howie's kitchen table enjoying decaf and a bagel. All is in place and proceeding well beyond smooth.

A REALLY GREAT FUNERAL

The clock next to his bed showed five-minutes to midnight when Howie was jerked out of a deep sleep by an ear-splitting crack and blinding flash of lightning, followed by a long, rolling tympani of thunder. It is just as well since Howie has to pee something wicked.

After tending to nature, Howie shuffles out of the bathroom and, before returning to his bed, peeks-in on his freshly kidnapped friend.

Just as Howie opened the door to his spare room, another flash filled the room, and in that momentary strobe of overpowering white light, Howie sees Max, spread-eagled, and face down, half out of the bed and onto the floor.

An hour later, Rocco, Sam and Noodles have arrived and are standing with a badly shaken Howie Brechmeyer, staring at Max's dead body.

"*DID YOU TRY TO DOING CPA, OR SOMETHING?*" Sam yelled.

"It's *R*. CPR! No, he was gone. Stone fucking cold. It was too late for any of that," Howie said, barely able to stifle a sob. "What the hell are we going to do?"

"We gotta call the police. We can't wait too long," Noodles said.

"Oh, shit…one of us got to go to Max's place and get that damn ransom note back," Howie noted, a slight catch of fear in his voice.

Noodles raised his hand. "I'll go."

A REALLY GREAT FUNERAL

"Don't forget to turn off the lights in the garage. And the garage door..."

"Yeah, I know. Close it."

The funeral home has one of those easily forgettable funeral-homey names, like *East Lawn,* or maybe it was *River Rest.* It hardly mattered. Dead is dead.

Seated with his friends at the rear of the sparsely-filled chapel, Rocco Capelli's calling it *Our Lady Of Ulterior Motives* is a typical bit of nervous, wisecrack, funeral funny business. His lame attempt to soften the sadness.

A week before, they had been five men of a certain age who'd met at a local health club and become good friends.

Now, one of them was in a thin pine box, at the front of the chapel, well on his way to becoming an urn full of ashes.

They fell silent when recorded organ music wafted from a speaker beside the plinth supporting Max's casket.

A side door opened and Max, Jr., his wife and son emerge and take seats on the front row. A female Rabbi follows, taking her position behind a Plexiglas lectern.

The music trails off to an uncomfortable silence as the Rabbi, an accomplished public speaker, stands quietly until she was certain she has the undivided attention of the small audience. Then, as any good actor would, she waits a bit longer.

A REALLY GREAT FUNERAL

On the outskirts of Bangalore, India, a spotless, hanger-like space housed an intricate warren of tiny cubicles. Each cube is equipped with telephonic equipment manned by a single operator. The operator's job is to make outgoing sales calls for whichever client happens to be paying for the service.

On this day a young woman named *Shatara*, which, in Hindu means umbrella, was making what are known in the *Tela-Sell* industry, as 'cold calls.' This particular assignment is hawking a revolutionary new ergonomically designed vibrating lounge chair called the *Snugulator. Shatara* is using a list of prospects, all of whom have one thing in common: Health club memberships. They should, by extrapolation, be interested in all things healthy, including a *Snugulator*, obtainable for five laughably low payments of only $99.95, plus shipping and handling.

She sips tea as she dials one of the random numbers.

On the first ring, a few dozen hands dive into pockets and handbags, and frantically pat clothing. Heads swiveled this way and that, searching for the guilty party stupid enough not to turn off a cell phone at a funeral.

A collective realization that no one in the sanctuary has the offensive sounding mobile phone, came quickly—something they should have known immediately, given the unique ringtone: a lively harmonica rendition of an old Russian Army Marching song.

But the four guys in the back of the chapel know instantly.

It's Max's phone.

Apparently, Max, Jr., had placed it—a little parting gesture—in the coffin with his father and it's now ringing.

And then the ringing stops.

And Max's recently recorded proof-of-life message plays—loud and barely muffled by an inch of cheap pine, drifts out over the audience:

"SON. IT'S ME, YOUR FATHER, MAX. YOU GOTTA GET ME OUT OF HERE, BUT IT MAY TAKE SOME CASH…"

The Rabbi lost bladder control.

Max's good-for-nothing daughter-in-law fainted.

Henry, Max's grandson burst into tears and would be in therapy for many years to come.

Max's buddies in the back row had never laughed so hard.

Any way you look at it — it was a really great funeral.

The End

Photo by J. E. Cohn

ABOUT THE AUTHOR

Mike Slosberg lives and writes in New York City. He is currently at work on a fourth novel, QUACKS, a medical thriller.

Titles by Mike Slosberg

Short Stories

TEN STORIES YOU SHOULD READ BEFORE THEY BECOME MOVIES

Novels

A BABY TO DIE FOR

THE HITLER ERROR

THE AUGUST STRANGERS

Humor

PIMP MY WALKER —
The Official Book of Old Age Haiku

All titles are available from the Author at www.mikeslosbergbooks.com, on Amazon.com, BN.com and many other websites around the world.

www.ingramcontent.com/pod-product-compliance
Lightning Source LLC
LaVergne TN
LVHW052340100826
845147LV00021B/1128

* 9 7 8 1 9 4 5 2 5 7 4 1 4 *